Twizted

By Seduction

by
Zoraida Fonseca

LOOKING BACK

After everything that Ivyon had endured she was blessed for her life and family. She always wondered what it would be like to finally have the sister she never had, at least one of them anyway. She always wondered what it would be like to have the father she never had. Now she knew what it felt like to have both. Since Kelli died, Ivyon, Bronte, and Derek became close. Ivyon would spend every other weekend with her father; they talked every day, and they became closer with every second. Ivyon and Bronte started a relationship she would have never thought possible. They went out on the weekends Ivyon didn't spend with her father, and like her and her father, Bronte and Ivyon talked every day.

Ivyon devoted herself and time to her new family, so she didn't have time to engage in her normal activities. During the past year, Ivyon had no time for herself; she hadn't even looked at a toy, let alone had sex. She had a hard time without family before; she didn't want to give it up again. She told herself that she would never be without a family again. Ivyon had different plans than sleeping around; she wanted to change that part of her life. She thought that if she spent more time with her family and did more for her business that she wouldn't take another walk down that road. For all she knew, she would lead a normal life.

She started to do normal things such as going to the movies, skating and shopping. She did all these things with Bronte. Ivyon was afraid to step foot into a club; she didn't feel as though she had enough willpower yet to not take someone home. She never really told Bronte why she didn't want to go clubbing anymore, she just told her that she always had bad experiences when she goes. Bronte didn't question her too much about it; she just kept quite about the situation hoping that one day Ivyon would come around.

Ivyon did share some of her past with her sister, but she left out the most important things. She told her how after a very long time she started to trust men again. She told her about Rufus, how he made her feel, how he made love to her, how she thought he would always be there for her. She told her that came to an end after catching him sleeping with someone she knew. She told Bronte how the ending of their relationship made her not want to trust men again. Bronte wasn't having that "every man ain't shit" bullshit. She had a plan to get Ivyon out of the house and dating again. Bronte didn't want to push her, so she would wait for a little while longer before trying to get her to go out.

In the meantime, Ivyon and Bronte were at the mall one day when they ran across Vici. Ivyon didn't know the first thing to do. As soon as she saw her, she started to think about the many days and nights they shared together. She started to think about their first time together and how she made Ivyon cum harder than any man she'd ever been with. Ivyon started to panic when she saw her. Her first thought was to walk in the other direction or just pretend that she didn't even see her. She knew that she had to speak to her; after all, this girl had been her best friend since her freshman year in college. She told herself that if Vici spotted her then she would speak but if not she would keep going.

"Ivyon?"

Shit, she saw me. What the hell am I going to do now?

"Vici, how have you been?"

"I'm good. How about you? I haven't heard from you in awhile! Is everything okay? I tried calling but I never get an answer."

"Everything's fine. You know I'm trying to get to know my father now, and I'm building a closer relationship with my sister Bronte. You remember her, right? I'm just trying to stay out of trouble."

"Ivy, you never were the type to get into any trouble."

"You know what I mean. I told you that I was going to calm down."

"You mean to tell me that you haven't been with anyone in what, a year?"

"Shh…Bronte doesn't know yet, and this isn't the way for her to find out."

"Ivy, I don't care what a girl is going through, you can't stop living! You have to have a good time, meet someone, go out, and have sex. Play with your toys, for God's sake. She shouldn't know about your past; you two are just getting to know each other anyway, and aside from that you are grown, which means you can damn well do whatever you want, and it's no one's business but your own. "

"Vici, you know you are my best friend, and I love you with all my heart, but I have to try to do right by me."

"You call this doing right by you? Ivy, what are you doing right? You never go out, you don't have a sex life, you don't even call me anymore. So please do tell how you are doing right by yourself."

"Look, I'm trying to do right with my family and my business, that's all."

"Ivy, when haven't you done right by your family and business? You've always done right by your family even though they took you for granted. You never let that get you down or come in between living your life. You've never let your personal life interfere with your business. Ivy, you are one of the strongest people I know, and trust me, I know many people."

"It's different now. I'm keeping in touch with my father and sister. Do you realize how much what I was doing could hurt them if they found out?"

"Ivy, you are a grown woman with needs, and I said before your life is your business. I'm pretty sure they lead lives of their own and trust me when I say that their needs come before you. Look let me take you out tonight and see if I can change your mind."

"I won't even let my sister take me out."

"I'm not your sister. Be ready at eight."

"Where are we going?"

"We don't have to go anywhere if you don't want. We can sit in the house and continue this conversation, we can go out to a club, or I can teach you how to love yourself again. It's up to you, you make the call."

"I'll let you know at eight."

"Don't stand me up Ivy. I'll never forgive you if you do."

"I won't, I promise."

This is exactly what Ivyon feared. She wasn't ready to go out and live again. She wasn't ready for how Vici planned on showing her how to be a woman again. She hasn't had sex in a whole year, she knew what Vici could do to her and she wasn't sure if she was ready for that again. To avoid having sex, she would have Vici take her out to show her a good time.

Ivyon knew she could trust Vici on not doing something she didn't want her to do, but she wasn't sure if she could trust herself on doing all the things she wanted Vici to do. So many decisions, heart racing, and goose bumps rising all over her body, Ivyon decided to take a hot bath thinking back on the time's that Vici and her shared.

One night in college, Ivy was feeling a little down and Vici knew just what to do to get her back up. Ivy was telling Vici that all of her life she never really felt loved how she didn't feel loved by the many men she'd been with, that she needed a full time man in her life. Vici took that and ran with it. She told Ivyon to lie down on her stomach, that she wanted to massage her back while they talked and Ivyon did what she was told. Vici started off with massaging her back, down her thighs, down to her calves and finally to her toes. She relaxed every muscle in Ivyon's body.

After messaging every inch of her body with her hands, she did it with her tongue. Ivyon thought she had died and gone to haven from the way Vici was making her feel. She had never felt as good as she did when she was with Vici, no man that she'd ever met could make her feel this good. Vici knew the state she put Ivyon in, she did it every time. She knew that she had Ivyon captivated, that she would let Vici do whatever she wanted. Afterwards Vici hand cuffed Ivy to each one of the poles of the bed. She traced small circles around each of her nipples, than she traced a line from her breast all the way down to her clit. Ivyon was on cloud nine, but Vici wasn't finished. She didn't stop there; she stuck her tongue in and out of Ivyon's pussy, making small circles around her clit as she reached it, making sure not to neglect it. Ivy felt so good she wanted to grab Vici's hair or scratch her back or something, but she couldn't she was tied up. The only other thing she could do was scream her name.

"VICCCCCIIIII"

Afterwards Vici took some massage oils and massaged Ivy's inner thighs and the center of her awaiting valley below. Vici left her there to catch her breathe as she had another surprise waiting for her, Vici got up and went to get a feather out of the closet to trace Ivy's body with. Vici just sat and watched Ivy try to get away from it, it was kind of cute watching her because it tickled so much and all she could do was stay there and take whatever Vici was doing to her.

Next thing Ivy knew, Vici put on some soft music and got on top of Ivy in the 72 position. Ivy had no choice but to give Vici some pleasure, it wasn't like she would object to it either. Vici had two fingers inserted in Ivy's ass while eating her pussy with her thumb inserted in her pussy. That shit was driving Ivy crazy, she couldn't hold her composure any longer, she stopped eating Vici and started to scream at the top of lungs from the pleasure she was receiving. Hearing Ivyon's appreciation for Vici's pleasure made Vici lick faster and finger fuck her harder.

Thinking about that night made Ivy start to touch herself, still in the tub, her head went back and she heard her own moans. She came so hard she forgot what she was missing. "Damn that was a good nut, I need more of that. Now I know what Vici was talking about."

A NIGHT OUT WITH VICI

"Shit, what the hell am I getting myself into? What the hell am I going to wear? I don't even know where the hell I'm going. Maybe I should wear a skirt, or maybe I'll wear pants. I'm not used to this shit anymore. Why in the hell did I tell her that she could take me out? Now my phone is ringing.

"Hello"

"Ivy, what the hell are you still doing in the house?"

"What are you talking about? It's not eight yet."

"Shit Ivy, its 7:30"

"Okay you act like you live an hour away you only live about ten minutes away."

"Ivy I'm making sure you don't stand me up."

"Where are we going anyway? I don't know what to wear."

"Where do you want to go? I told you it was up to you."

"Okay, I haven't been to a club in God knows when, so let's go to the club."

"Then you know what to wear, I'll see you at eight. You know it's too early to go to a club at eight so what do you want to do until we go to the club?"

"I'll figure that out when I get there, I got another call on the other line, I'll see you in about ten minutes."

"Hello"

"What's up, you trying to go out tonight?"

"I've got plans tonight, sorry Tay."

"With who, you don't even go out with me. Where are you going?"

"Hold up on the questions, I can only answer one at a time. I'm going out with Vici and I don't know where we're going just yet."

"Why in the hell didn't you tell me? You know this is our weekend."

"Well I'm sorry, Vici and I haven't been out in a year and I haven't even seen or talked to her since then so I owe her this."

"Well I hope you have a good time and I want all the details. Ivy, please enjoy yourself, you don't do anything anymore ever since you found us. You didn't have to stop your life because you found us. You could have still been doing the same things."

"I know that Tay, but I didn't want to lose you again. I mean we haven't seen or heard from each other in about ten years or more."

"Just know that I love you for who you are and I want you to be happy no matter what. So enjoy yourself, I'm not going anywhere, you're stuck with me now."

"I love you too, Tay. I'll talk to you tomorrow."
Time to get dressed, if I know Vici she's got some shit up her sleeve. I'll put on these low rise shorts, deep V-neck shirt and my knee boots. This shirts hangs down on my shoulders so I can show cleavage, I hope these shorts will hug my ass like I think they will. Everything is perfect, now should I wear my hair up or down? I think I'll wear it down, that's even sexier, having my hair go straight down my back. All I need now is some perfume and I'm ready to go. Shit Vici's going to kick my ass, it's already eight.

"Damn Ivy it took you long enough, it's fucking 8:20."

"Vici I'm here now, we don't even know where we are going. You look good but not better than me."
This hussy had on some mother fucking gauchos, some knee boots and a low v-neck shirt, low enough to hang over her shoulders to compliment her breast. Which it did very well, she would definitely have heads turning.

"Vici, you're supposed to be taking me out to have a good time, so how you going try to look better than me?"

"I am taking you out to have a good time, but I got to look good to."

"Whatever ,Vici! Where are we going anyway?"

"Since we are dressed for the occasion I guess we are going to the club.

"Let's go get something to eat first."

"Girl, you always want something to eat and don't gain a pound."

"Don't hate."

"Whatever. Where do you want to get something to eat from?"

"I want to sit down and enjoy it."

"So where the fuck do you want to go?"

"Let's go down Moe's and then hit H2O."

"Ivy, that's a lot of driving."

"You said you were taking me out to have a good time. Let's go, I'll help you do the driving."

"Why H2O?"

"Different dance rooms!"

Once at the club Ivyon and Vici sat at the bar to observe. Vici had the plans to let Ivy get lose and enjoy herself. No pressure from her, everything was up to Ivy. Once Ivy had about three Remy & Coke's she was ready for the dance floor. Ivyon had her eye on one guy the entire time she sat at the bar. Like she always said, she could tell the way a man fucked by the way he moved his hips on the dance floor. The good part about it was, they were in the Reggae room, so of course you know that this man was moving his hips.

"Instead of watching how he moves, why don't you go over there and help him move?!"

"What are you talking about Vici?"

"Ivy, I see you watching him, go join him."

Ivy took that as lead way and went over to join him. Ivy walked up to him from the back so he wouldn't see her coming. She grabbed his hips to let him know that she was there, he never even turned around and they just rocked to the beat. The DJ rocked a slow grinding jam next which allowed the gentleman to turn around to face Ivy and rock her slow.

"Just what I wanted, now I could really tell if this man could fuck and do it right. He held me close and grinds me slow and sensual. I want this man so bad my pussy is getting wet from the way he felt against my body."

Ivy thought to herself about what she was about to do.

"I really want this man but I said that I wouldn't do this anymore for the sake of my family. What the hell am I talking about, I don't have any kids and I'm grown. I can do what I want. Fuck it, I got to see what he's about, I haven't fucked in over a year, time to see if I still got it."

Ivyon reached down to grab at his manhood, but was stopped in her tracks by his hand.

"You seem like a very nice lady, I don't want it this way."

"You don't even know me to determine if I'm a nice lady or not. Besides, any man in his right mind that's not gay would be happy to be in your current position."

"You are right, but pussy is thrown in my direction everyday so it's not like I'm missing out on something. It's just that you are too beautiful to give it away like you are trying now."

"Thanks for the complement but, you don't know the half of it."

"Like I said I know that you are too beautiful to be giving it away like you're trying to do now. Why are you trying to give it away anyway? If you were my woman, I wouldn't even allow you in a club. You wouldn't want for anything, because everything would be right at your finger tips."

"You talk a good game, but I don't want for anything nor do I need anybody to do anything for me."

"Well take my number and let me show you. If you don't mind me asking, why is it that you feel that you don't need anyone to do anything for you?"

"I don't need anyone to do anything for me, I know I don't. I own three restaurants and working on my forth, I take care of myself."

"That may be true, but you still need someone to love you. What is success without having someone to share it with? Are you truly happy owning three restaurants?"

"Yes, I am. Wait a minute, why are we even having this conversation anyway? You act as though you know me that well to know what I need."

"I know that every beautiful woman needs a man by her side, even if she owns her own business, even though she takes care of herself."

"Like I said before, you talk a good game."

"Ivy, what are you doing? I've been looking all over for you!"

"This young man was just telling me how beautiful I am, that's all."

Ivyon gave Vici a look that said "get me the hell away from here". Vici knew exactly what that meant.

"Well I'm ready to go."

"Okay, let's go. Nice talking to you"

"You do need a name with that number, unless you truly don't plan on using it."

"I was so caught up that I didn't even realize that he slipped his number into my hand. Where are my manners? I'm Ivyon, and you?"

"I'm Winston. Do you have a business card or something?"

"I'll give you a call. It has been nice talking to you."

Ivyon walked away pissed off about the fact that she couldn't get at least a quickie. She had never been turned down before, so this was definitely a first.

"Ivy, what the hell was that, I told you to go dance with him, not make love to his ear."

"Vici that has never happened to me before, maybe I'm losing my game, I've never been turned down before."

"Ivyon you didn't lose anything, he just doesn't have any idea what he's missing out on. I would love to taste you and you know that all you have to do is say the words."

Ivyon didn't know what to say or do about that because she knew exactly what Vici was capable of. I would really love to have my pussy ate right now, but I don't know if I'm ready for Vici at this time. I'll never know if I don't get past my fear, I know she wouldn't hurt me but I just might enjoy it a little too much.

Vici knew something was bothering Ivyon by the look in her eyes.

"Ivy, what's wrong?"

"Nothing, what makes you think something's wrong?"

"I can see it in your eyes that something's bothering you. Are you sure you're okay?"

"Yes, I'm just ready to go. I can't believe I just got shot down."

"Where do you want to go?"

"What's out in the movies?"

"Ivy where the hell do you expect to catch a movie 12:30 at night, we'll just go home and watch a movie that way we can catch up on all the lost time."

"Well let's just have a drink for right now, I don't want to spoil your night."

I knew this would happen, maybe she does just want to talk or maybe she has something else in mind. I'll never know until I go home. Shit all of these fine ass men up in here and I can't get not one. I guess I'll just call it a night and go home. Who is this man that keep's looking me in my face? I wonder if I know him, he does look kind of familiar especially around the eyes. Oh shit I know this can't be who I think it is. Shit it is Rufus, I got to get out of here, I hope he doesn't realize it's me. Fuck he is coming this way, maybe if I turn my back on him he'll keep walking.

"Hello Ivyon."

"Uh, Ivy I'll catch up with you later."

VICI

"Look at her over there acting like she don't want to talk to Rufus, he was her heart. That man could have made her climb a mountain even thought she's afraid of heights. Well shit I'm looking good tonight, she's in safe hands so I'm going to make my way to the dance floor to see if I can catch a man."

"I already see someone that I might take home with me tonight. I'll play it cool, act as if I don't see him coming this way, I'll put on a show for him. The perfect song is playing too, Tweet's "Ooops." As the song was playing I grind my hips and swayed back and forth while I let my hands roam all over my body. I slid my fingers through my long hair to give me a better affect that'll make him make his way over here to me. I'll turn my back on him now to let him know that I know he's watching and that it's alright. Now if I'm playing this right he should be walking up behind me right about now and wrap his arms around my waist and rock slowly with me.

"Um you smell so good and I love the way you move your hips, it's like you are Tweet."

"Thanks, now be quit and just dance."

"I knew what I was doing; now it's time to see if he can keep up with me. If he can, he may just get lucky tonight. The DJ must have read my mind, I'll be damned if he didn't put on Chris Brown's "Take You Down". As I throw my ass into him and pulled away, he was there to my catch and counteract my every move. He turned me around, dipped me back and looked into my eyes. Pulling me back to him, he grabbed my face as he pressed firmly into my body and ran his fingers through my hair he gripped my hair and made me sway to his beat.

I know for sure that he is going home with me, there's no question about that. Goddamn he just made me cum all over my panties just by dancing with him. I am speechless, the only thing I can do is let him guide my body the way he wants and look into his eyes because as bad as I want to take him down, I don't want to mess up this moment. I don't know how much more I can take; I think it may be time to go. The DJ is really taking it back now; he threw on "Red Light Special" by TLC. That is the right song for this moment because baby is in for a red light special.

"How about we leave and go somewhere to be alone."

"You must have ESP; I was just thinking the same thing."

Ain't this some shit, shorty is up on his game he came correct before I could. I am going to fuck his brains out tonight, oh Lord I just hope he can fuck as well as he can dance.

"Give me one second, I came here with my best friend and I have to make sure she'll be okay."

"Okay, sure go handle your business. Just don't keep me waiting too long or even worse, run away on me."

"Oh I'm not going anywhere except with you."

I got to find Ivyon, hopefully she'll go home with Rufus. I need this just as much as she does. I don't even know if she's where I left her, I'll find out real soon.

"Vici, I just ran half way around this club looking for you. Where were you?"

"I was just looking for you. Is everything okay?"

"Girl yeah, I just wanted to tell you that I'm going home with Rufus, he wants to talk somewhere quietly. We both know what that means."

In unison they said, "He wants to fuck."

"That's good, I was looking for you to tell you that I found this nice guy that I talked to and dance with to about three songs and now we're thinking about dipping off too."

"You be careful, when you get outside text me with his tag number and address."

"You already know, I want all the details too, no holding back."

"I won't, same thing goes for you."

They gave each other hugs and kisses and went there separate way.

I am so glad Rufus didn't piss her off and I know that it's nothing more that Ivy wants than to fuck the shit out of Rufus. Shit, I know I would. Well I can't be worried about that I've got my own piece of dick waiting on me tonight.

Now I just have to find mister man and hope and pray that he's just as good in bed as he is on the dance floor.
Walking to the opposite direction I can see him against the wall, hopefully waiting on me. I'll walk behind him so he doesn't see me coming.

Grabbing him from behind, "I told you I would come right back."

Turning towards me he said "I'm so glad that you did I was starting to think that you weren't coming back."

"I wouldn't miss out on this night for anything."
Thinking to myself if Ivyon needed me I would have been shit out of luck and hopefully he would have given me a raincheck.
"So where are you parked?"

"I'm parked around back, how about you."

"I'm around back also."

Walking out of the club together all Vici could think about was having the time of her life with this man. I mean all she knew about him was that he could dance she didn't even know his name. She didn't know if this man was a serial murderer or what. He could have been a rapist or anything for that matter, she didn't care about any of that all she wanted to do was have the fuck of her life and that's what she planned on getting.

"So what's your name?"

"Vici. what's yours?"

"Nice to meet you Vici, my name is Bryan."

"Ok Bryan how far do you live from here?"

"About 10-15 minutes, do you want to leave your car here or did you want to follow me?"

"I think I'll just follow you, I want to leave and go home straight from your house and not have to come pick up my car from somewhere."

"That's fine."
He just doesn't know that I'm going to text Ivy with all his information just in case he is some kind of murderer. If he is, I hope he fucks the shit out of me first.

Once back at Bryan's house I was in heaven, from the way he touched me to the way he kissed me, to the way he ran his fingers through my hair and the way his tongue danced around my body, I knew I hit the jackpot with Bryan. As I walked into the house he followed behind me and once inside he wrapped his muscular arms around my small frame and began to kiss my neck, gently sweeping my hair from one side to the other trying not to neglect the other side. "Aw," was all I could hear from my own lips as I felt his hands creep up the center of my stomach to my breast and to my erect nipples. Making circles around my nipples with his fingers caused me to spill another "Aw" and what I was feeling was so relaxing.

I let my head fall back as he reached under my chin to pull my face closer to his as he let his tongue trace my lips. He came from behind me now standing face to face so close that I could smell what he had for his last drink. He stuck his tongue deep into my mouth and my eyes rolled in the back of my head….this man sure can kiss, I thought as I tasted the remainder of the dark and smooth Louis XXIII on his tongue as it intertwined with mine and did a dance of their own while I felt my insides melt.

Ordinary this night started because I wanted to make Ivy feel like she was on cloud nine again, to get her to remember how beautiful she is, and that she always make me cream in my pants so I know she'll make a nigga rock hard, but of course that didn't happen so I gotta go with plan B. This is almost as good, I came back to reality once he started to glide my shirt over my head, once it hit the floor he came in close, pulled my hair to let my head fall back and started to trace a line from my neck down to my nipples. From there he looked deep into my eyes and asked "are you ready to be taken to ecstasy?" The word "YES" escaped my mouth before I even knew it, Bryan undid my pants and let them slip to floor as he picked me up and placed my back up against the wall. He looked deep into my eyes while he massaged my clit with his thumb and fucked me with his middle finger until I came all over it.

From the moment he felt my walls tighten and my juices release, he dropped to floor to catch all the cum and fucked me with his tongue and made small circles around my clit until I came again. By this time he was rock hard and my mouth was watering from the thought of having his dick in it. As he stood from eating my pussy, I dropped to suck his dick, I first teased the head by making circles around the outer ring and flicking my tongue back and forth across the urethra. I traced the shaft of his dick with my tongue until I reached his sack, I placed both his testacies in my mouth and played with them with my tongue to get him to relax. When I saw his head go back, I went in for the kill; I placed one hand at the base of his dick as my mouth surrounded the shaft. I stroked him up and down in a circular motion with my hand as my mouth followed suit and my tongue in the opposite direction around the head of his dick once I came up. I continued this for five minutes until he came in my mouth. Once he erupted I never stopped until he was erect again, once I got him to where I needed him to be, I walked him to his couch and pushed him back. I reached in my purse and got a condom and I put it on him with my mouth once that was in place I got right down to business. I straddled him from behind and rode that dick while he pulled on my hair and played with my clit at the same time. As I came down on him he pumped harder inside me, he grabbed me by the hips, pushed me forward to touch my toes and gave me the business.

I'm glad I came home with this man, I haven't been handled like this in a very long time, and I loved every minute of it. Once I came from being in this position, he picks me up and carries me to the kitchen where he places me on the counter top and fucks the shit outta me. The shit was so good, I'm scratching his back, pulling on the faucet, biting my lip, curling my toes, screaming and pulling my own damn hair until we came together. Of course being the woman that I am I got his number afterward so we could hook up again, this was definitely the best fuck I've had in a long time.

IVYON

"Hello Rufus."

"How have you been? I haven't seen you in a long time, you left so suddenly."

"Oh you mean after I caught you fucking somebody on the desk in your office? That wasn't sudden and you're lucky that's all I did."

"Look can we talk about this? It doesn't have to be this way between us!"

"Rufus you said everything you could when you were on that desk assed out with another woman."
I looked into his eyes before he could even get out another word and I walked away. I left him there calling out for me and out of nowhere here comes Josh; he walks right up to me, slides his hand underneath my hair to cradle my neck and kisses me deeply right there in the middle of the dance floor, in direct eyesight so Rufus could see. After this deep kiss of seduction, he pulls away slowly and locks eyes with mine and as I give him a slight smile, I looked back at Rufus and back at Josh, then walked out the club with my arm wrapped in his. That stunt he pulled was right on time and I wasn't mad at him for doing it either that was the highlight of my night. Josh was someone from my past when I was in college that I thought I was in love with after Vici and I had our episodes. Josh was older and he graduated before I did, things didn't work out and we lost contact. I ran into him once after that and we had a night of

passion that was remarkably memorable, and from there we lost contact once more.

"Sorry about that but you looked like you could use some help. Then again I'm not sorry, but how have you been?"

"I didn't think you were, but I've been okay. Longtime no see; how have you been?"

"I thought I was good until I just saw you and I realized I've been settling."

"Whatever, you think you are so smooth. I haven't seen you in about two years; I probably never came across your mind."

"I'm sorry if you feel that way Ivy, I think about you often. But that's for another time. So tell me about yourself, what have you been getting into lately? I've had the honor of dining in one of your restaurants."

"Well I had some ups and downs but for the most part I've been blessed, I've finally met my father. My mother and oldest brother passed away last year, and my sister and I are getting close, so all is well. What a coincidence running into you like this, are you always going be my knight in shining armor?"

"I can be that and much more if you'll let me!"

I didn't even have an answer for that, I just smiled and looked away.

"So where are you headed now?'

"Well since Vici left me, I guess I'm going home."

"Vici? Why does that name sound familiar?"

"You remember Vici, my roommate from college."

"Oh that Vici, wow you guys are still good friends, huh? That's good to still be friends after all this time."

"Well actually she's my best friend; we've been through hell and high water together."

Josh and I sat right there for about two hours and just talked about the past, present and what could be our future before he asked if I wanted to go to his house and finish our conversation. Needless to say I took my ass right over there hoping that that's not the only reason he asked me over. When we got there he dimmed the lights, put on some slow jams, and retrieved a chilled bottle of Chardonnay from the kitchen. We continued talking about the good times as well as the bad and about two glasses of wine later, I found myself kissing and undressing him. Josh grabbed me by my face and looked deep into my eyes like at the club and asked "Are you sure this is what you want?" I looked at him sternly with lust in my eyes and replied, "YES."

From there he cradled me in his arms and carried me to his bedroom and laid me down on his king sized bed, lit some cradles, turned on the radio, and got some baby oil from the closet. He walks over to me and said "whatever you don't want to happen won't, but I promise I will treat you like the queen you are." With that I just closed my eyes and let the man work. I felt him slowly undressing me from head to toe, he didn't leave a piece of clothing on my body, he kissed my lips slow and soft, then he traced kisses from my neck, to my breast, to my stomach, down my thighs, to my calves, and finally resting with my feet where he showed extra attention to my toes by sucking each and every one of them. I felt goose bumps on my entire body as this man was taking me to ecstasy. He took a feather and ran it across my whole body before pouring baby oil down the center of my body. He let his hands slide up and down the front of my body giving me a pleasurable massage from head to toe. When he got to my womanhood, he parted my lips and massage oh so gently with his tongue in the inside before massaging the outside and then in my inner thighs. After my front was done he told me to turn on my stomach as he continued with my treat, he treated my back side with the same precision and gentleness. I felt like I'd fallen in love all over again. When he reached my ass, as he parted my cheeks, before doing so he asked if he could taste me. Little did he know I was ready for him to taste me the moment we walked in the door, I replied, "YES." OH MY GOD, I'm experienced in what I do but never before have I felt pleasure like this. This man ate my ass and pussy from behind while finger fucking me in each hole at the same time and never once let an ounce of cum drip down my leg, and I came from both holes.

I was so relaxed I didn't have a care in the world. This man made everything go away, the only thing that mattered was that time and place. With everything he did, he asked my permission first and the next thing he asked was if he could enter me from behind. I was so waiting on this part so I replied, "YES." To my surprise he did exactly that, he poured more baby oil down the crack of my ass and massaged it in all over my ass and pussy. He must have rubbed some on him as well cause the next thing I know he was going right in my ass with ease, and I don't really fuck in the butt but I let this man have his way with me. I thought it was gonna hurt so I tensed up, and he said to me "just relax and you will be ok, if you want me to stop I will." I let out a deep sigh and I let everything go, I relaxed every muscle in my body and I felt a pleasure I never felt before. I thought to myself if this man asked me to marry him right now I would, that's how good he made me feel. After about ten minutes of that he pulled out and entered into my pussy like I thought he would the first time, while he's stroking me from behind I feel a vibration on my asshole, and he asked "can I insert this?" I replied "YES" not knowing what I was getting myself into but I let him. He stopped stroking me just for a second to insert this vibrator in my ass. He turned the vibration off at first so not to give me a surprise all at once. Once it was in he turned the vibration back on and continued to stroke me. I had double penetration with a little extra and needless to say I came so hard my whole body shook and a single tear dropped from my eye. This is by far the best sex I've ever had, this even tops Rufus.

I felt like I should do something to please him as well so when he asked me to turn over, I reached for his dick to put in my mouth and he stopped me.

"You'll have plenty of time for that on another occasion but now your every wish is my command, I'm here to please you".

All I could say was "ok." He got up and turned the shower on and asked me to join him, once in there he kissed me passionately and dropped to one knee, placed my leg on his shoulder and he tasted me all over again. Once I came again he wrapped my legs around his waist and he fucked me against the wall under the shower head and I came twice more before he washed my body from head to toe. He asked was I satisfied or do I want more, I told him I was satisfied but with a grin on my face. So he asked me do you want me to continue to make love to you or would you like me to fuck you? I had to think about it for a minute, he just made love to me now I want to know what it's like for him to fuck me, and I replied "I want you to fuck me." Once those words left my mouth it was on, he grabbed me and put me on top of the sink and fucked me good, after about five minutes of this he carried me back into the bedroom, threw me on the bed and turned me around. He had me climbing walls the way he was hitting it from the back. He would spank me, pull my hair, talking shit and all and I was loving every minute of it until he finally came. This man got stamina, he can really go and he never once worried about having an organism, his whole objective was to please me. We lay their in bed not saying a word until he fell asleep, when I knew for certain he was asleep I put on my clothes, left my number on his nightstand and went home. I wondered if Vici got lucky that night cause I damn sure did, I shouldn't have lied to her about going home with Rufus though. Although, if he would have said the right things, I sure as hell would have gone with him, no worries though, I had the time of my life with Josh.

I really did believe that Rufus was the love of my life, the one to make everything better for me, the one to put an end to it all. All I wanted was him, I never once wanted another man or woman for that matter while I was with him; unfortunately, just like the many men of my past and the one's I hear about, one woman just wasn't enough for him, he had to go and be greedy. I was happy with him, I saw myself settling down and marrying him, maybe have a kid or two. This man was my dream, until he turned out to be my nightmare. I really need to find Vici, I need to talk to her.

BRONTE

I'm so happy that Ivyon is going out to have some fun, she really needs it. I know she thinks I don't know about her past, but shit the apple doesn't fall too far from the tree. I've been keeping up on her private life since I met Tina. That is one crazy chic, and she was totally obsessed with Ivyon. I remember it like it was yesterday.

I was at my best friend's birthday party looking sexy, sensual, sophisticated, and tempting all at the same time. Next thing I know, she walks up to me and we lock eyes, she sits next to me and order's a drink, all the while making small talk with me. She smiled at me and told me I looked very sexy, and I thanked her for the compliment. The bartender walked over and sat her drink in front of her, and she never took her eyes off me. She turned to pay the bartender with a soft grin on her face; she turned to look back at me, took a sip from her drink and winked her eye at me.

All I could do was smile, as I could not take my eyes off this woman. She places her drink back on the bar and as she gets up to leave, she walks up to me and glides her hand up my arm, once she reached my breast, she tucked a small piece of paper between my breast and she mouthed the words, "call me if you're interested, I promise to be gentle".

I could not believe what I was hearing, a woman coming on to me and so strong. I've never had this happen to me before. By this time I was more than interested, I was intrigued and excited. I sat there at that bar for 10 minutes with thoughts of this woman on my mind. I was confused as to what to do; I've always played around with the thought of being with another woman, but never really had the courage to do so.

I never even noticed my best friend walk up behind me, she tapped me on the shoulder and told me to go out on the dance floor to have some fun. I guess I was sitting there too long. I went out to the dance floor and danced to a few songs. About an hour later, I walk over to the bar and ordered a "fuck me against the wall", I downed the drink and I was soon headed to my car. I'm sitting in my car nervous as hell, my palms were sweaty. I took the piece of paper from out my cleavage and unfold it and to my surprise, her phone number and home address was there.

Nervous at first, I convince myself that this is what I've been wanting to try for so long and just never had the guts to. It's either now or never. I pick up the phone and dial the number, the phone rings once and I'm ready to hang it up when all of a sudden I hear, "I'm in the bubble bath, door is already unlocked", and then the line went silent as she hung up the phone. Contemplating what to do next; I had to show up after I already called her, but how did she even know it was me? I played around with the idea of should I go or not, finally making up my mind, I rush right over there. To my surprise, as I opened the front door I was caught off guard by the candles that were lit in every inch of the house as the sounds of jazz serenade my mind and

caress my body as if it was my lead in the forbidden dance as I danced to my own tune.

I quickly come out of my trance realizing what I was here to do. Palms sweaty once more as the thought ran through my mind. I start to walk up the stairs and in my nervousness; I could hear the sensual sound of my stiletto heel meeting the hardwood floor as I make my way to her. I have butterflies in the pit of my stomach, and I run across the thought of just turning around to leave.

I get the courage to keep going and once I reach the top of the stairs, the sight in front of me was breathtaking. Butterscotch skin, slender legs, long brown flowing hair pulled back into a ponytail, firm C cup breast with milk chocolate nipples, bubbles sliding down the center of her body. All I could do was stair at this portrait in front of me, I never heard her say anything to me, I just saw her fingers gesturing for me to come closer.

That was the longest walk I've made in my life time. Once there, she reaches out to me and caresses the side of my face, and pulls me into her. She plants a soft kiss on my lips, waiting for my approval to go deeper. Never receiving it, she does it again, this time sliding her sweet peach tasting tongue between my lips, and I gratefully opened my mouth. She kissed me deep and slow, this was no doubt the best kiss I've ever had in my life. She pulls back from me and I'm left there, eyes closed, mouth open, waiting for her next move. I didn't feel anything but I hear the sound of water, so I open my eyes to see her stepping out of the tub, dripping wet of bubbles and water. She moves behind me and she kneels down caressing my legs all the way up to my shoulders. She plants a soft kiss on my neck, and whispers "may I?" In total shock, not even realizing I could speak, I let out the word, "YES".

She unzipped my dress and let it fall to the floor, revealing my red lace thong and bra; she kisses me across my shoulder and stands in front of me to ask me if she could taste me. I nod my head yes out of sheer lust, she guides me to her bed where she lays me down slow and lies on top of me. She kissed my neck and behind my ears where she then whispers "everything will be okay". She plants soft kisses all down the center of me body and asked me to stand, once I do she removes my bra and panties but leaves my candy apple red stilettos on. I'm so nervous at this time that I'm shaking. She senses this and she tells me "if you want me to stop I will, but I promise you if you let me continue you will not be disappointed. I will not cause you any pain; I will remove it from existence as I take you to ecstasy." I take a deep breath and I start to relax, I reach to remove my glasses and she stops me and says, "No."

She wraps her hand around my throat and she starts to lick, kiss and suck down to my nipples. She took her other hand and stuck her index finger into my mouth, naturally I start to suck on it, and she inserts another, and I do the same. Making circles around my nipples, she looks up at me and winks. She takes her fingers from out my mouth and inserts them into my wet, moist, warm, awaiting valley below. I let my head fall back and let out a breath. Back to my ear, she asks, "Would you like me to stop?" I whisper, "No," with that she looks at me and smiles.

She drops to her knees and spreads open my legs, she licks up and down my inner thighs as she thumbs my clit. I'm in heaven as she licks the center of my slit back and forth while still playing with my clit with her thumb. Coming up for air briefly, she turns me around to eat me from behind. Oh my goodness, I was lost in time, standing still in frame. I just could not believe what I was experiencing; never would I have thought it would be like that. She told me to turn around; she wanted to see my face. I did, and the expression I gave was full of approval. She went back to tasting me this time with so much intensity, I shook, I grabbed at the sheets, I wrapped my thighs around her head, I bucked and I screamed, I damn near fainted as she brought me to my first lesbian orgasm. She stopped long enough for me to catch my breath and to relax the tension in my body. She asked me would I like to be penetrated, eyes still closed, I told her at this point I didn't care what she did. I was in heaven and I did not want to come back down.

Next thing I knew, I felt her hands very slippery and warm as she caressed the inside of my lips and thumbed my clit. Out of nowhere I felt the mouth of my valley being opened by an erect penis, certainly not hers, I looked down and to my surprise she had on a strap-on. If I previously thought it couldn't get any better, I was wrong. She stroked me nice and slow at first allowing me to wrap my mind around the events. Then she asked me to ride her, and oh boy did I, and I climaxed so hard. We tussled in the sheets for hours as we satisfied each other and she took me to new heights. I never felt that way before in my life, and I was hooked, I never wanted this night to end. Sadly it had to come to an end. I made sure we exchanged information before I left, seeing as how I wanted her to make me feel this way over and over again. Oddly, I asked her name, and she said to me "I think it's more intriguing and sexy if we didn't exchange names." With that she kissed me and said good night.

I thought that was kind of strange, than again the entire night was strange. A stranger approaches me in a night club, seduces me, gives me her number, invites me over and gives me the best orgasm I've ever had in my life. I have never in my life experienced this type of love making before, and from that moment on I wanted it every minute I could have it. Thinking about it now is making me horny, I want to call her up right now. Every encounter we shared after that was intense just the same; it was like we just met all over again.

We did eventually exchange names, she told me her name was Samone, but never used them while we made love. It was just sexier this way, we kept suspense in it. We made arrangements one night to meet at the National Harbor about 3 in the morning, I just had to see her so I called her up and she met me there. I lived fairly close so I was there waiting for her in my sheer teddy covered in a blanket. She walked up behind me, wrapped my hair in her hand pulling my head back towards her and kissed me so passionately.

I came to my knees to face her and I kissed her with just as much passion. We rolled around in the sand, feeling the cool summer breeze caressing our bodies, becoming entangled within each other. My moans met hers as I took control of the situation for the first time. I caressed the center of her body with my hands and traced her silhouette with my tongue. I gave her passion that I never knew I possessed. I came just from the pleasure I knew for sure that I was giving her. I lay on top of her in between her legs as I fingered her until she climaxed over my fingers. I took them from out of her and I let her tasted herself as I suckled the remaining of her from her lips.

I got up and walked over to the "Awaking" statue that's lying in the sand, she follows closely behind me. I lay my warm body up against the cold steal that makes up his hand and I propped my leg on one of his fingers, all the while motioning her to come to me. I tell her to get on her knees to taste me, take her time and put two fingers inside of me. We carried on like this for hours, me tasting her while she lay in the mouth of the statue, we scissor each other in the sand where the "Awakening" torso should have been. We were in heaven with each other, we were beyond cloud nine, and we exceeded ecstasy.

It was nothing for us to get together and have the time of our lives. It was normal, something we both needed, something we both wanted, and something we both had to have. Our love making went on like this for months, no complications, no interruptions, no disappointments just great sex.

TESSIA

After so many years of being single, Tessia was in desperate need of a man. She pretty much stayed single after having her husband thrown into jail, after she practically walked in on him raping Ivyon. Tessia knew in her heart that calling the cops that night was the right thing to do; any mother would have done the same. So she made the sacrifice of having her life or saving Ivyon's, she chose the ladder. She thought back on her entire relationship with her husband, and realized everything she ever knew or thought she knew about him; about them was a lie and it was so horrific for her to figure that out. It's been a year since she'd been with anyone; her heart was naturally still with her husband being as though that's the only man she'd ever been with her entire life. Starting a new relationship would be too difficult for her to trust again. However; every girl needs to get her feet wet every once in a while, and that's exactly what she planned on doing. Now who she was doing it with was a whole different story, she just had to make sure to be very careful not to let a certain person find out.

"Tessia, this is Derek, my father. Derek this is Tessia, my mother." Ivyon introduced them to each other in hopes they would share the same interest at heart, which obviously is her. She loved them unconditionally for just being who they were to her, she hoped that they could love her the same. Tessia and Derek locked eyes sharing in a secret language that only they would become fluent in, a communication that only they could understand. Their initial introduction came a year earlier, after Ivyon found Derek allowing her to build a relationship with him.

Following that introduction was something neither one of them were expecting, but something both of them accepted and have been sharing ever since. After their brief introduction, Derek stole Tessia's attention and asked if he could speak to her in private whenever she got the chance. Captured by his persona, Tessia fell into a comatose like phase, not being able to comprehend anything. Clearing his throat, "um, um, um" Derek asked again, "Excuse me, Tessia, when you have a chance, could I speak to you privately?"

"Oh, please forgive me Derek, I must have went on a day dream. What was it that you asked me?"
Derek let his eyes find the floor as a slight blush came across his face, and he asked again. "When you have a chance, can I speak to you in private?"
"Please forgive me, sure we can speak in private. Can you just give me a few minutes to freshen up? I won't be long I promise."
"Sure, no problem."
Tessia walked off to clear her mind and gather her thoughts. Nothing to be worried about, she was sure that Derek could want nothing more than to speak with her about Ivyon, that was easy, she could handle that. This man made her feel like a woman again, she was starting to feel things that she hadn't felt in a very long time. Tessia freshened her perfume and make-up not wanting to take too long and keep Derek waiting. When she got back to him, he was awaiting patiently for her in her living room. Thoughts roaming all over the place, nervous and not knowing what to expect from the conversation, Tessia braced herself for what was about to come.

"Tessia, I never really had the chance to thank you for taking care of Ivyon during her desperate times of need.

Trust me, had I known Ivyon was living in turmoil, I would
have stepped in a long time ago to take her away from this
nightmare; however, sadly enough for whatever reason, be
it selfish or logical to Kelli, she kept me away from Ivyon.
Sheltered her from me, never let me see her, not so much as
to even talk to her. I knew nothing about what my daughter
was going through, and I blame myself for that. I should
have been more of a man to Kelli and definitely more of a
father to Ivyon, I should have stepped in no matter what
Kelli said. All Kelli had to do was contact me, if it was too
much for her. She knew I would have come to get my baby
girl. Ivyon would have never had to suffer the way she had,
had Kelli just picked up the phone, wrote a letter even,
anything."

Derek rambled on and on, losing Tessia briefly along the
way. He was hurt as much as any father who thought he
had failed his children would be. Tessia placed her hand on
his cheek, motioning him to sit down with just the warmth
of her touch against his face, she whispered the words
"Derek, you cannot beat yourself up for something you
knew nothing about. I understand that you are hurting, that
you wish you could have rescued her from all of that, but
there was no way you could have known. I'm sure Kelli did
whatever she did thinking it was the right decision, you
can't hold yourself accountable for that."

Derek understood where Tessia was coming from but yet
he couldn't allow himself to be cut any slack. He was in
pain from all the hardships his daughter had to encounter,
what hardships turned her into. If those things never
happened to her, she could had a completely different life.
No doubt in his mind that she would have still been
successful, but not with the cost of being addicted to sex.
He realized that things can happen every day that could be
out of his control, but had he had the chance to provide for

his daughter, there stood the chance that none of those bad things would have happened to her.

"Derek, there is no need to revisit the past and bet ourselves up about it, let's just be thankful that we were put in her life when she needed us most even though we would have wanted to be there from the beginning to prevent this. Everything that happens in life is already written, she didn't need us then even though all of us may think that she did. Ivyon went through those bad things and look how wonderful she turned out to be. We have a daughter that we can be proud of. She has her life together, she has everything a young woman like herself could ask for and she's living her life. Let's just be grateful of that."

Tessia's words touched Derek in a way he never thought possible. He looked at her with astonishment in his eyes and did the first thing that came natural to him. He reached up and slid his hand underneath her hair, cupping the back of her neck, bringing her in closer to him to kiss her pink powdered lips. A kiss so sweet couldn't possibly be anything else. Tessia gratefully accepted his offer by relaxing her shoulders and falling into his embrace, lost in time and in each other their kiss lasted what felt like an eternity, but couldn't have possibly been no more than mere seconds. Breaking away from the kiss, touching her lips, Tessia felt alive again for the first time in a long time. She looked at Derek who offered his apologizes and before he knew it, Tessia leaned in to kiss again; this time with more aggression and passion. They were seep in a passion either of them could explain, lost in a body language that they both were engaged. Their kiss turned into a succulent dance of seduction, hands caressed body parts and traveled the unknown. Lost in each other, Derek forgot that he had a wife back home in California; the life that he knew was the furthest thing from his mind. The temperature started to

heat up between them, and all of a sudden, the realization
that he did have a wife waiting for him back at home
invaded his thoughts of pleasure, causing him to stop in
mid motion, he said "Tessia, I am so sorry. I don't know
what's gotten into me; I have a wife back home in
California waiting for my return. Clearly I have lead you on
and for that I apologize, I over stepped my boundaries; I
don't know what has gotten into me. Again, I'm sorry,
would you please forgive me?"

"Derek don't apologize, you acted on the moment and I
simply reacted, and for my part in that, I apologize. I
should have known better, Ivyon has mentioned to me in
the past that you were married, I guess I just let my own
selfish thinking take control of the situation.
"Tessia, don't be so hard on yourself, we both acted in the
heat of the moment for whatever reason, so there's no need
for you to beat yourself up about it. How about I take you
out to dinner to offer my apologies, does that sound like
something you would be up for?"
"Sure, why not? But only if I'm paying."
"No way, what type of gentleman would I be if I let a
beautiful woman such as you pay for my dinner? I believe
my mother taught me better than that."
"Well if you don't let me pay for it, it would make me feel
as though we were on a date. How about this, we choose a
nice restaurant to dine at, drive separate cars and we pay
Dutch? That way neither of us feels awkward about going
to dinner and fighting over the check. What do you say, do
we have a deal?"
"Okay, sure we have a deal, but only if it makes you feel
better."
"It really would. Have you ever been to any of Ivyon's
restaurants?
"You know, surprisingly, I never have. I should be
ashamed of myself."

"Well that makes two of us; I guess we both should feel ashamed. Maybe we should make one of them our destination?"

"That sounds like a plan to me. You pick which one and give me a call and I'll meet you there around 8 pm tonight. Is that too late for you to be out?"

With a light chuckle and a slight smile, Tessia simply replied, "Last time I checked, I thought I was grown."

With that, the date was set. They both wanted to skip the date and have each other for dinner right then and there; however, Derek had a family back at home that needed him, and Tessia needed a man full time. They looked into each other's eyes as if they were reading each other's minds, knowing what the other wanted, but resisted the urge. Tessia got up from the couch, walking to the door with Derek in tow, they agreed to meet each other later that night for dinner and drinks to smooth over any uncomfortableness that they may have been feeling, hoping to put this evening behind them.

DEREK

The thought of Tessia kissing me made me feel things I haven't felt since my night with Kelli. I felt alive again, needed, like I was the only man that mattered to her in the world. Nothing can ever replace that feeling, and that feeling alone can make a man feel as though he can conquer the world. Knowing that you're needed or desired just does something to your ego, it makes you feel things that you've never felt before, and that's exactly how Tessia made me feel. Meeting up with Tessia tonight may be a bad idea, but she has something that I need. Something that I yearn for, it's calling out to me. I want her with everything inside me. I don't want just to make love to her, I want her to feel me in her soul, I want to be irresistible to her.

I know that this is wrong in every way imaginable, me having a family back at home, and getting involved with the only real mother Ivyon has ever known. However, I am a man with needs, and I need her. Laura is wonderful to me, she provides me with everything a husband could need or ask for, and it's just something about Tessia that is going to make me step out of my marriage. Could it be the fact that she is lonely? Is it her beauty? Is it her innocence? What could it be that is drawing in to this woman? I don't know, but what I do know is that I will soon find out. She wants me just as bad as I want her. I won't force myself on her; however I will lead the way. I'll open that door and if she follows then I won't feel so bad.

All this and more ran through Derek's mind as he changed clothes in his hotel room, awaiting the time to meet Tessia at the restaurant. They agreed to go Dutch, but little did she know, Derek was a total gentleman no matter the circumstances, he would not allow her to pay for her meal or any other meal for that matter. His plan was to wine and dine her, to open that door of ecstasy that they shared. The heat between them was rising and he wanted so badly to put out that flame, and he just knew she felt it too.

Derek was always an early bird, so naturally he reached the restaurant a full 20 minutes ahead of time. It was a nice cool, calm night out, so he figured they'd have dinner on the roof top. He made his way to the roof to check the area, once there he found that even if it was winter out, it was still nice enough to dine on the roof. Ivyon had this place decked out to the fullest; no wonder she always received great ratings. The roof top was totally enclosed by glass that could be opened at any time to give the full effect of being outside. There was candle light everywhere and fresh flowers to follow. This place was only thought of in your dreams, yet Ivyon had made it come true. The table tops were made of marble to give you that warm feeling, and the floors were polished stone. This place truly was to die for. Derek found the manager and made arrangements for them to be seated in a certain area of the roof top. He looked over the menu, choosing everything they would eat from appetizers down to the wine they would drink with their dessert. Not knowing if Tessia ate any of what he picked out, he was a man of taste, so he took it with stride.

Eight o' clock sharp, Tessia made her entrance into the restaurant where she was escorted by the maître d' to the roof top. Tessia had no idea what kind of surprise she was in for, all she knew was that being in a public place with this man was the best thing for the both of them considering how their evening took off earlier. She respected the fact that he was a married man, and she would never want to cross that line, however, this man

made her feel things she hadn't felt in so long. He made her
dream again, made her feel a wetness she thought had soon
dried the moment her husband was taken away. She felt
sexy again, like a woman that someone actually wanted,
that alone was worth sleeping with Derek. She didn't want
to hurt anyone in the process and she surely did not want to
risk Ivyon ever finding out, if she and Derek decided to do
anything. The best thing for her at this moment was to just
sit down and have a nice dinner followed by nice
conversation hopefully and let the evening go. That's what
she planned to do, just put everything behind her since she
knew there was no future in it anyway.

When she reached the roof top of the restaurant, she was
astonished, she couldn't believe her eyes. The place was
immaculate, even more beautiful than the inside. Couples
were sitting happily together, enjoying in each other's bliss,
seemingly so happy together. The atmosphere was so
serene, so exotic, yet innocent. So sexy, yet calm, there was
no disturbance here; it held a welcoming feeling that made
you never want to leave. Tessia was in a whole new world,
way out of her league, this was a place for lover's, they
probably should have occupied a table downstairs with the
normal dining parties, Tessia thought to herself. This put
her in a place of harmony and love-making, something that
she wanted oh so badly, this was all wrong for her, if she
indeed intended to behave herself and not seduce this man
or let him seduce her. Well I'm here now, she thought as
she walked toward Derek who greeted her standing by her
chair with a smile on his face. She kept telling herself that
all she had to do was remain calm, keep the conversation
out of the direction of sex, and maybe concentrate more on
Ivyon. Of course this would be hard for her to do
considering the atmosphere, how she was feeling, and oh
dear God how this man was dressed and smelled. He
smelled of heaven, and she could have sworn she had just

died and gone there. It would be extremely hard for her to behave when all she wanted was to feel this man inside her. Just the site of him standing there in front of her was causing her insides to tingle, creating an even flow of warm, explosive wetness to travel down her tunnel causing dampness in her panties. Approaching Derek, he greeted her with a kiss on her cheek before pushing her chair in, all she could do was cross her legs and twitch. Derek noticed the sudden change in her posture, and smiled to himself, knowing that she wanted him just as much as he wanted to her.

"Tessia, how are you this evening?"

"Derek, I'm doing well. Thanks for asking; How about yourself?"

"I'm doing pretty well actually. I hope you don't mind, but I took the liberty of ordering everything for you. Considering this is a night of apologies, I thought I'd better make a lasting impression."

"Derek, you didn't have to go through all of that. We are on common ground, there's no need for anymore apologies. Even though it's an awesome gesture, you didn't have to go out of your way."

"Out of my way? Trust me; it isn't out of my way. I've started you off with a grape martini for your drink and we'll share a crab and lobster imperial dip for an appetizer. Following that, you'll have roasted duck topped with a rosemary glaze, red potatoes and sautéed spinach. After that, if you're up for dessert, we'll have a warm apple crumb cake topped with French vanilla ice cream and shaved almonds. I hope I've done a great job at selecting dinner for you. How does that sound?"

With a smile as wide as the ocean, Tessia replied
"Mouthwatering; I've never had a man order my meal for
me, especially not as well as you have. I cannot wait to
taste all of what you've just mentioned. I'm sure it'll be
enough to stuff me for the next three days." They shared in
a laugh before the waiter came over with Tessia's drink
along with their appetizer.

Breaking the silence between them, Derek asked Tessia to
tell him all about life with Ivyon. She began with the first
day they met how she saw so much hurt and
disappointment in Ivyon's eyes all she wanted to do was
endure the pain for her. To swallow it up, erase it from
existence. She explained to Derek that Ivyon told her just
once of what had happed to her and she made her promise
to never speak of it again, and she made that promise and
hasn't broken it yet. Ivyon was a very strong young
woman, even as a little girl when she first came to Tessia.
She was forced to grow up early and learn how to take care
of herself, but Tessia never crowded her, she never treated
her like a child, or a victim, and over the years, Ivyon has
grown to appreciate that about Tessia, that's what made
their bond even stronger. The evening went on like this
with them sharing stories and getting to know each other.
Time had escaped them and before they knew it, 3 martinis
and 2 glasses of wine later, it was after midnight. Derek
offered to drive her home but she wouldn't hear of it, so he
followed her there to make sure she got there safely. They
both pulled into her driveway and he saw her to the door.

"Derek I want to let you know that I had a ….."
Before Tessia could finish her sentence, Derek reached in
and kissed her so deeply and full of passion that she could
not refuse him. This was of course what they both wanted,
even it was wrong. Wrong or right was the furthest thing

from their minds at the moment, all Tessia could concentrate on were her moans from the way this man was making her feel. The only thing on Derek's mind was his perturbing penis as he kissed her and she kissed him back. She hadn't refused him as he thought she would and that alone turned him on.

Derek backed her into her house where he took a handful of her breast and massaged it gently, never taking his tongue out of her mouth. After massaging her breast, he caressed the center of her body until he reached her valley below, once there he could feel the heat emitting through her panties, as well as the wetness. He teased her clit by rubbing the fabric of her panties against it back and forth, back and forth. He watched her as she let her head fall back and he let out a soft moan, this gave him even more satisfaction for himself. With every moan she gave, he was drifting further and further away, losing control of the situation, almost wanting to skip the foreplay and go straight to the "fucking"; however, he didn't want to cheat her nor himself. Derek watched her facial expressions as he continued to stroke her clit, watching the muscles in her face change position every time he stroked her differently, he began to kiss, lick, and suck on her neck creating more pleasure for her. She lifted her leg around his waist, grabbed his wrist and forced him to put his fingers inside her. She guided his hand in the direction of her G-spot, once found she erupted in wetness all over his fingers and in her panties. She hadn't cum so hard in God knows how long, and all she could think of was that she wanted it again.

Seeing how this made her react, Derek took that and ran with it. He would insert one finger at a time into her tunnel until he had in all four, and he created a rhythem inside her, bringing her to the edge of her cliff and just before she would jump causing eruption, he would pull his fingers out and suckle on 2 to taste her essence allowing her to suckle the other 2. He did this for the next 10 minutes over and over again, causing her to lose her breathe a couple of times, bringing her back to reality. After he was satisfied with her amount of pleasure, he picked her up, wrapping her legs around his waist; he carried her up to her bedroom where he placed her on the bed. Lying her down slow and gently, Derek reached under her dress giving her panties a slight tug in order to get them off, he put the crotch of her panties to his nose and took a deep breathe. Derek dropped down to one knee and dove head first into her dripping pussy, causing Tessia's back to arch and her fist to ball up the sheets in them. She was in heaven; she hadn't felt this way in so long, she forgot how good it felt. Little did she know, Derek was enjoying this more than she was, he was a man that got off by making his woman feel good.

Five minutes later, Derek came from between her legs, pushing her dress up with his hands while they caressed her thighs and his tongue traveled to the center of her body meeting her mouth, she kissed him as he pulled her dress over her head. Derek looked down at Tessia as if looking for reassurance; she looked him in his eyes and kissed him once more. She reached down to undo his belt, sliding her hands under his shirt to see exactly what his body would feel like. She slowly unbuttoned his shirt and slid it down his arms. Taking in the view she was given, she was in aww, awaiting the pleasure she knew she was sure to receive. Tessia kissed his chest and down to his stomach, undoing his button on his pants, Derek stood and let them fall to hit the floor. Penis standing at attention, Tessia couldn't take her eyes off it. Sliding to the edge of the bed, Tessia took all of Derek into her mouth with no hesitation. Her mouth gliding up and down the shaft of his penis, her hands gripping at the base, providing the control she needed in order to make his eyes roll into the back of his head. This was sort of an audition for Tessia, seeing as how she hadn't had sex in years, she wanted him to remember this moment, and she definitely needed the memories for herself in case she didn't receive this type of attention for a while.

Receiving a blow job that made his toes curl standing up, Derek had to feel the inside of her valley. He was nearing the point of eruption, and he wanted to make sure she received as many orgasms as she could stand before he released his. Pulling Tessia from the base of his penis, he picked her up, wrapping her legs around his waist, his penis had no trouble finding the passage way of her tunnel, as a matter of fact, he was greeted with a very warm succulent tight hug pulling him deeper inside for satisfaction. Placing Tessia against the wall of her bedroom, she arched her back each time he thrust forward, tightening the muscles of her vaginal wall as he pulled back, causing him to near eruption. Derek maintained his composer, pleasing Tessia was his number one goal, giving her as many orgasms as her small body could possibly handle would give him a satisfying orgasm and he could wait all night to reach his. The things Tessia was doing with her body was surely making it difficult for him not to explode.

Thrusting forward, Tessia wrapped her legs tighter around his waist, squeezing her muscles as tight as she could as Derek retracted his member from her secret garden, catching the head of his penis and swallowing it inside her, she held on as tight as she possibly could, creating the only option go forward or to stay still. Derek took the option of going forward in small strides, back and forth as much as Tessia allowed him, because at this point Tessia controlled the show, the action, the movement and the orgasms. Not

being able to control himself any long, Derek whispered to her,
"Are you ready for me to cum or would you like to cum more?" Tessia was in pure ecstasy, she could care either way, she hadn't felt this good in so long she was slowly losing control of her body. Losing count of the amount of times Derek has made her cum so far, she couldn't ask for anything more. Her body had never felt this way before, not even in the fifteen years of marriage had she felt as good as she was feeling within that moment. Tessia never wanted this moment to end, and neither did Derek, nonetheless, the feeling of pure pleasure, ecstasy, excitement, and heavenly bliss was slowly pushing his juices up the tunnel of his manhood. Tessia could not mouth the words to tell him to stop or keep going, so he read her face. Her face said that she wanted, that she needed, she desired, she demanded more.

Derek lifted Tessia from the wall, pulling himself away from her; he threw her on the bed on her stomach. Wrapping his arms around her waist, he put her on all fours, making her back arch toward him. One hand gripped around her midsection, he slowly licked her up and down her spine, sending chills through her body. Tessia threw her head back in excitement, Derek reached forward grabbing a handful and wrapping it into a fist, he pulled her head back slightly so he could see her face, "How bad do you want to feel me?"
"Derek, please, I want you inside me, I want to feel the earth shaking under my feet."
Derek took that and ran with it. He entered her with just enough force that would make her jump, but not enough to hurt her. Hair still wrapped in his fist, he took that as leverage, pulling her hair and grabbing her waist so she could feel all of him. He pounded in and out of Tessia for what seemed like forever, giving them both an earth

breaking orgasm. When he erupted and she came with him, the force was so powerful they fell from the bed onto the floor in exhaustion. Looking into each other's eyes, not with a sense of guilt but with satisfaction; Word's didn't need to be exchanged as they shared in something that was just as rare to the both of them; the evening was concluded, knowing that they could never give this up. An agreement made with only the language that the eyes could speak.

IVYON

Ivyon was finally getting her feel back for sex after the night she just had. She felt so good about it she wanted to call Vici immediately to tell her.

"Vici, are you busy today?"

"No. Why, is everything okay?"

"Yeah, everything's fine, I just wanted to have sort of a girl's day. I was wondering if you could come over and talk. I can make us a couple of drinks; I just went out and bought that new Peach Ciroc that I've been dying to taste."

"Sounds like fun. I hope you're going to cook something to go with it? You should call me over for dinner like you used to. What ever happened to that?"

"Girl you are a mess, you always want something to eat. When do you ever eat besides when you're over here?"

"That's the only time I eat, girl you know you got to feed me. I want some of that lemon pepper salmon and garlic potatoes that you are famous for and I'll be there around 6 tonight. Oh, and honey do I have a story to tell you."

"Yeah, well I have one to tell you too. See you at 6 sharp."

"Oh really, I wonder what kind of story this will be?"

"You'll just have to wait and see."

Ivyon starting preparing her dinner waiting for Vici when all sorts of thoughts just started to flood her mind…Damn I really miss Rufus, I wish it was him that I was cooking for instead of Vici…

She stopped and threw her head back trying to stop the tears from falling; however, one escaped and traveled a lonely road down the center of her cheek and landed in the corner of her mouth. Wiping the tear away, she screamed out, "WHY DID YOU BETRAY ME?!"

Screaming at Rufus even though he wasn't physically there, she still felt his touch all over her body, heard his voice with every thought and felt his breath on the nape of her neck as she felt his embrace spooning her in bed in the middle of the night…I loved you with all my heart and you go and cheat on me. I gave up my life to solely be with you, and I loved every moment of it. You made me whole; I needed for nothing or no one. You were the center if my universe, and now my world has disintegrated."

The more Ivyon talked, the more time got away from her. Not even realizing that her dinner was done, Vici walked right up on her, gaining entry using the spare key Ivyon had given her years ago.

"Ivy, who the hell are you talking to? Is everything okay?"

Tears streaming down Ivyon's face, she looked at Vici startled at first, and then she turned to walk away. Vici followed close behind her, calling out to her.

"Ivy, don't shut me out, you're my sister. Tell me what's going on, you know no matter what it is, I'm here for you. Ivy, talk to me, you're scaring me."

"Vici, I'm alright. I was just thinking about Rufus that's all. I really love him, it just hurts so bad that he would go and do that to me. I know he loves me Vici, I saw it in his eyes, but the fact still remains that he fucked that crazy bitch Tina."

"Ivy, I know sweetie but from what you told me, I don't think he did it intentionally. I think it's just like he said, she came in and seduced him, practically raped him honey."

"I know, but damn Vici, he couldn't fight her off? This shit is so hard, all I've been through and I finally settled down and learned how to love again…UGH. How could I have been so dumb? I loved every waking moment that I spent with him. I missed him every second that we spent apart."

"Ivy, if you feel like this when you're not with him, then why don't you just go back to him? Stop putting yourself through this pain and go get your man."

"Vici, it's not that easy, I…I…, well anyway, tell me about your night or whatever your greedy ass came over here to tell me."

Laughing, Ivyon tried to end the conversation and start a new one, hoping that Vici would leave the conversation alone. As much as Ivyon hated to admit it, she knew Vici was right. She did want Rufus back; she just didn't know how to swallow her pride to get her man back. She didn't want to seem weak; she didn't want him to feel like cheating on her was okay or acceptable. She desperately wanted to be back with Rufus but he hurt her too bad. The bruises in her heart were already so deep; she thought she'd die if she took another hit to the heart. Vici just looked her best friend in her eyes and felt all her pain, she wished it was something that she could do to make Ivyon feel better.

Vici really felt Ivyon's pain and knew that she couldn't and didn't want to talk about it anymore, so she changed the subject.

"Well when I left the club with Bryan, I knew I was in for a treat. Girl I got to his house and I had a blast. This man rocked my world; I haven't had good sex like that in so long. I left there well satisfied and wanting more, so of course we exchanged numbers." Vici managed to say all this while packing food in her mouth. "Girl this salmon and potatoes is hitting the spot, and what did you mix with this Ciroc? Enough about me, what did you want to talk about?"

"I mixed it with some Chardonnay and white grape juice. Anyway, as you know, I didn't go home with Rufus, instead I left the club and went home with Josh. He actually saved me from going home with Rufus, I wanted to so badly but I was playing tough. Anyway, Josh and I talked for a while about the past and what could have been, and in his eyes, what could be. Vici, he made love to me so sensual, I almost thought I was with Rufus again. Nobody had ever touched me like Rufus had, and I missed that so much. Yet I was getting it right there from Josh. I left there feeling so confused, I almost wanted to start something with me, but my heart belongs to Rufus."

"Damn girl, that's powerful."

"Vici, why does this have to be so hard? I mean I wanted to spend the rest of my life with him, I actually still do, but I don't know if I can bring myself to trust him again. Anyway, Josh handled me so gently, he took me to heights I only thought Rufus could; however, I still imagined it was Rufus that I was feeling. Josh had my body, but Rufus definitely occupied my mind, heart and soul. Damn just thinking about it is making me horny."

"Shit, you made me horny."

Ivyon looked at Vici, took a sip of her drink and walked toward her. Vici not knowing what to expect said "keep telling me how he loved you up." Ivyon bent down and put her hand on Vici's cheek, before kissing her, she said "I'll show you."

Vici had been waiting for this moment for over a year, but she didn't want to push herself up on Ivyon considering all that she'd been through. She willing accepted Ivyon's kiss and she almost took over the show, but she reminded herself that Ivyon was the one hurting and she would be there for her.

"Ivy, are you sure this is what you want to do?"

"What? You don't want me anymore Vici?"

"Honey I would give anything in this world to have you to myself, I just don't want to take advantage of you."

Ivyon still straddled on top Vici on the couch looked deep into her eyes and said "looks like I'm taking advantage of you."

Vici said no more, she let out a deep breath and let Ivyon have her way with her. Ivyon took Vici's shirt from over her head, cupped her breast and licked her neck. Vici let her head drop back as she prepared herself for an orgasm only Ivyon could give her. Ivyon laid Vici across the couch as she licked a line down her chest to her belly button, making circles around it. She reached under her and held

Vici's legs up to take off her panties from under her skirt. Ivyon took the panties and shoved them in Vici's mouth and took Vici into her mouth. She licked and sucked on Vici's clit and stuck her finger in her now dripping wet pussy. All she heard were appreciative moans escaping Vici's mouth. Ivyon knew she was doing a good job. She kept eating until Vici reached the edge of her climax; she convulsed and pulled at Ivyon's hair. Only for Ivyon to pull away just before Vici had the chance to explode. Vici looked in confusion at Ivyon waiting for an explanation.

"I don't want you to cum yet. Come with me."

Vici followed Ivyon to her bedroom where Ivyon took Vici's skirt off and told her to get in the bed. Ivyon blind folded Vici and tied each of her arms and legs to the bed post of her sleigh bed. Ivyon kissed Vici and told her to relax. Vici heard Ivyon moving some things around but had the slightest idea what she was in store for.

"I'm going to give you the time of your life."

By this time Vici was excited and could not wait to climax. She heard a vibration and knew that Ivyon was about to get freaky. Little did she know, Ivyon had a machine that delivered the most powerful vibrations and the maximum of pumps. Ivyon oiled Vici's pussy and placed the dildo inside Vici and turned the machine on high. She watched as Vici screamed and convulsed and finally climaxed. Once she reached her orgasm, Ivyon climbed on top of her face and demanded that she eat her while she was being fucked non-stop by this machine. Ivyon road Vici's tongue for all about five minutes until she reached her orgasm, she climbed down and turned the machine off and undid Vici's restraints.

"Goddamn Ivyon, where and when did you get that machine? That thing gave me a run for my money; we have to do that again."

Ivyon just smiled at her and Vici kissed Ivyon and gently pushed her back on the bed. She got on top of her in the 69 position and they feasted on each other. After making Ivyon climax again, Vici got up and went to Ivyon's closet; she pulled out her 10 inch strap-on and told Ivyon to get on all fours. Ivyon did what she was told and Vici inserted her from behind and unbeknownst to Ivyon, Vici had her bullet as well and she insert it into Ivyon's ass while she was hitting Ivyon in the doggy style position. After Ivyon came, Vici took the bullet out from her ass and put in her pussy, and while she fucked Ivyon in her ass with the strap-on. Ivyon was receiving pleasure from every end, and she didn't want it to stop. They continued giving each other the pleasure they missed well into the middle of the night before retiring to tell each other how much they've actually missed each other.

Rufus was the furthest thing away from her mind at that moment, but Vici knew that he had her heart and that she would never have Ivy the way she wanted her. She cradled Ivy as they lay in bed talking until Ivy fell asleep in her arms. Once Vici knew she was asleep she whispered into her ear,

"Ivy, I've loved you since college but I had to let you find your way. That may have been my greatest mistake as I realize now that your heart belongs to Rufus. However, I gained a wonderful best friend. I'll always be here for you, and I will not stand in your way to get Rufus back. Just know that if you ever realize you don't want to be with him, I'm here waiting. I love you."

With that Vici kissed Ivy behind the ear and eased out her bed to get dressed and leave for the night. Ivyon felt Vici get out her bed to leave and she wiped her tears from her eyes. She wasn't asleep and she heard everything Vici said. She wished she could have told Vici that she felt the same way that she wanted to be with her, but Vici was right, her heart truly did belong to Rufus, and she could not move on until she tried to make it work with him.

TINA

Tina sat out in the street as she watched Vici drive down Ivyon's driveway and out through her gates. This was Tina's only chance to get into Ivyon's house without invitation, she knew she would never get Ivyon to invite her over but she had to make Ivyon see that she was truly in love with her. That she was the best person for Ivyon, she would love her unconditionally, and give her whatever she wanted.

Tina snuck inside the iron gates just as Vici pulled out of them, and made her way up the driveway. She was hoping that Vici left the door unlocked, Tina never thought the plan entirely through. If Vici hadn't left the door unlocked, what was Tina going to do? She couldn't break in, and she would be stuck inside the gates until Ivyon decided to leave, and it was no telling when that would be being as though Ivyon was her own boss. Tina got to the door, and it was locked. A defeated Tina didn't know what to do next, as she sat there thinking about her next move.

Tina sat on Ivyon's marble steps for all about 10 minutes before she saw the light in Ivyon's room come on. Tina hid in the bushes not wanting Ivyon to see her. She watched as Ivyon came on to her balcony and stared into the sky. She saw her crying, shaking her head. She was talking but, Tina couldn't make out what she was saying. She started to cry hysterically, Tina wanted so bad to console her but she couldn't go to her like this. Tina just sat and waited for the right time.

Ivyon cried for about 10 minutes before she went inside to take a shower. To Tina's surprise this would be her way in because Ivyon didn't close her balcony doors behind her. Tina waited for about three minutes, trying to give Ivyon enough time to actually get in the shower. Tina climbed up the column to reach the balcony. Once there she walked around Ivyon's room embracing it all, this was her first time ever being in Ivyon's house, let alone her room. Ivyon had class; she had hardwood floors all through her house from what Tina could see. In her master bedroom she had a full sized bathroom with a Jacuzzi tub surrounded by marble, the tub was so high, there were three steps you had to climb in order to get in it. There was a separate stand up shower with a Kohler shower system installed, at least 4 shower heads on each of the three walls that surrounded her and also the ceiling above her. These features were accompanied by a huge his and hers sink with bright vanity lights across the top.

Her bedroom had a king sized sleigh bed with a three step stoop to use to climb in and sheer drop curtains that surrounded her bed, shielding her from the outside world. In the right corner of the room there was a glass vanity set with all kinds a perfumes ranging from Bvlgari, DKNY, Chanel, Usher, and Versace, just to name a few, along with a wide variety of lotions. In the left corner of the room sat a white chaise all by itself with a caramel silk scarf draped across it. In the center of the floor lies a snow white plush rug that was soft as pillows.

Tina wanted to surprise Ivyon, she knew that she wouldn't just be welcomed with opened arms. She had to come up with a plan quick. Tina lit candles all around Ivyon's room except the corner she occupied. She had soft music playing and that same caramel scarf she saw sitting on the Chase, she now had it lying on the bed. Tina sat there in the nude waiting for Ivyon to step into the room. Once Ivyon came into her room, she jumped and screamed out to Vici. Holding her chest after being scared, she said

"Vici?"

"Shh…pick up the scarf on the bed and tie it over your eyes."

Walking towards her Ivyon said "Vici, I thought you were gone, when did you have time to come back and do all this?"

Tina yelled out "STOP. Shhh Ivy, put the scarf around your eyes and climb into bed."

"Okay, but why are you whispering and sitting over there in the dark?"

"I want to have some fun, now be quiet and let me take care of you."

Ivyon had no idea that this wasn't Vici. She thought maybe Vici wanted to come back and finish what they stated not knowing just how much time she would have with Ivyon before she went back to Rufus. Ivyon had no objections, she didn't want to be alone that night anyway and besides she enjoyed what they shared and she wanted more.

Once Ivyon tied the scarf around her eyes and lay in bed, Tina walked over to her and smelled her hair and then kissed her cheek, and then softly planted a kiss on her lips. Tina reached for Ivyon's arms and pinned them down over top her head, keeping Ivyon from feeling her features, so she would know she wasn't Vici. With her left hand she cupped Ivyon's breast and sucked on her nipple. Nipple in her mouth she let her hand creep down to her valley below when she roughly inserted her four fingers.

Ivyon jumped. "Vici what the hell are you doing? That's too damn rough."

Shhh. Ivy I won't hurt you."

Seeing the scarf Ivyon wrapped her hair with at night, Tina snatched it and forcefully tied Ivyon to her bed post. She sank down between Ivyon's legs and forcefully pushed them back so she could get at her pussy better. Tina started to eat Ivyon slowly at first, but she got so caught up in it, she couldn't believe she finally had the chance to have Ivyon again and at her mercy. Tina lost track of what she was doing, she inserted one finger at a time into Ivyon's valley until she had her entire fest in. She forcefully pounded in and out of Ivyon, not even realizing that she was hurting her. Ivyon screamed out to her to stop, but Tina could not hear her, she was in a crazed trance, all she wanted to do was be with Ivyon.

Ivyon twitched and turned trying to get out of her restraints. Finally she got one hand free and she snatched off her blindfold. Looking down, pissed that Vici was being so rough with her she screamed at her, "Vici, what the hell are you doing?"

Ivyon would soon be in for a rude awakening, she reached over to get her other hand free, and she reached down to grab at Vici's face and soon realized it was not Vici.

Squinting her eyes to see just who was between her legs. In shock Ivyon couldn't believe what or who she was seeing. Hoping she's seeing things, Ivyon rubbed at her eyes in disbelief.

"Tina?"

Tina started laughing at her and this enraged Ivyon. Tina had broken into her house and portrayed herself as Vici and sexually assaulted her. Pretending to be Vici the entire time, Ivyon was infuriated; flames grew in her eyes as she jumped toward Tina in an attempt to strangle her. Tina ran around the room screaming at Ivyon that she loved her and she only wanted to make her happy. She didn't mean to be so rough with her while they were making love; she only wanted to please her. Tina somehow managed to get away from Ivyon, running down the stairs and out the front door. Ivyon grabbed the phone to call the police, she would have Tina arrested for breaking and entering, and sexual assault. Ivyon quickly thought about it and decided not to call the cops; she would deal with Tina on her own terms. Obviously the bitch was sick and twisted.

Ivyon knew Tina couldn't get from out of her estate unless she became Spiderman and climbed her iron gate. Ivyon ran back upstairs to her room, inside her walk-in closet, on the top shelve in a cherry-oak wood box she retrieved her 40 caliber, 23 series, 13 clip Glock. Ivyon desperately ran down those stairs naked in an attempt to catch Tina before the crazy bitch somehow managed to get over her gates. Just as Ivyon reached her 10 foot long porch, Tina was indeed climbing the gate trying to get away. Ivyon took aim at Tina and let off 2 shoots, but both were a miss. Tina frantically climbed the gates to get away before Ivyon shot her. Making it over the gate, Ivyon reached for the phone to call the police to make a report, but she didn't instead she called Bronte.

Bronte lived in Prince Georges County, Maryland while Ivyon lived in Pennsylvania. That had to have been between a 4-5 hour drive for them to reach each other. Neither of them were willing to take that drive in the middle of the night, Ivyon just told Bronte everything that happened. Bronte couldn't believe that "Tina" was still crazy enough to mess with Ivyon after Ivyon beat her ass in the hospital.

Tina left Ivyon's house in a hurry. She jumped in her car and headed straight to the hospital. Little did Ivyon know, she had shot Tina right in her leg as she was going over the fence. Tina got to the hospital and once they saw she was a gunshot victim, they called the police. When the police arrived, Tina gave them some fake story that she was leaving a bar and fight broke out where they were shooting and she just happened to get shot as she was walking to her car. She didn't see her shooter because there was a crowd of people and chaos everywhere. The police believed her story and told her if she could remember anything to just give them a call.

Tina lay up in that hospital bed laughing, wondering how she could get Ivyon the next time without hurting her. Tina didn't think anything was wrong with her and what she was doing, all she knew was that she wanted Ivyon and she would do whatever and whoever she had to do in order to get her.

TINA

Tina was the definition of crazy, as a matter of fact, she was beyond crazy, and she was Ludacris. As a teen, Tina had many mental issues, ranging from as far as schizophrenia, bipolar disorder, to having multiple personalities. Tina was a mess, she came from a family that was too proud, one that didn't accept the truth too well and did whatever they had to do to cover it up or keep it from getting out. Tina's mother studied her entire educational life over in another country, Asia to be exact. See Tina's mother came from a wealthy family; her family had what you would call "old money". To give you a better idea of what I mean, think about the Queen of England and the money they have. Tina's family had so much money that they didn't even spend it, wherever they frequented, everything was always put on a tab for them, just their name alone, got them anything they wanted, from homes to luxury cars.

Tina's family was one of the very few black family's within that category, which of whom were very well respected people. It appeared they were in some sort of secret society, the untouchables. No one would dare mess with them or try to double cross them. They could run a red light in front of a cop and instead giving them a ticket, the police would stop traffic for them to get through, they were beyond powerful.
During her senior year of high school over in Asia, she met another American, whom she adored, his name was Timothy. They soon became best friends, forming an unbreakable bound that only they could share as they saw themselves as outlaws. They were the real foreigners there

in Asia studying to be much more than any of their peers would imagine. Shirle had no other choice but to befriend Timothy and he had no choice but to befriend her. They were all alone in a foreign country even though Shirle had spent most of her life there, Timothy was the new guy on the block and she had to show him the ropes.

They never spent a minute apart outside of going to sleep for the night. They did home assignments and projects together, after school they would always take an hour walk and talked about life and family back at home, he was from North Dakota while she was from New York. He had all books smarts, while she had a mixture of book and street smarts. She taught Timothy how to get out of trouble and to get into some trouble too. During some of their free time together, Shirle taught him everything that she had already known about the country and the language. They were the best of friends; all they had was each other.

Shirle and Timothy were set to graduate at the end of the summer, and that meant going back home to New York for Shirle, but Timothy was to stay and get his college degree there also. On graduation day they were so excited to finally be finished with school and to get the chance to go home. They sat out in the crowd of all the other kids waiting to hear their names to be called so they could go up on stage and finally receive their diplomas. Shirle's name was called first; she jumped to her feet, ran over to Timothy and gave him a hug as she looked into the crowd for her family. She didn't see them, so she made her way to the stage, once more looking over the crowd to find her family, listening closely to see if she could hear cheers in her honor. There was none, she looked out into the crowd with disappointment weighing heavy on her heart, just as she was turning her head back toward the principal, she locked eyes with Timothy and let a tear rolled down her cheek.

Her focus turned back to the principal as she wiped what she thought to sure be the last tear she would shed over her family. Coming up on the principal, she received her diploma in one hand, and shook the principal's hand with the other. She smiled a faint smile and walked off the stage, watching all the other students repeat the same actions as she previously had, only difference was their family were there to cheer them on and let them know that they have accomplished something major. She waited until the ceremony was over and Timothy was cleared from his family, they walked to her dorm room hand in hand quietly, not a word spoken between them. Shirle knew what she had intended to do, that night she was going to give her virginity away. She was tired of being let down by her people that was most important to her.

Shirle decided to live life the way she wanted to from then on out. She would be going home in a week and Timothy would be leaving also. She wanted a moment to remember, they reached her dorm room and she invited Timothy inside. He was hesitant at first but he followed her in. Once inside they sat on her bed, holding hands looking at each other, waiting for the other to make the first move. Neither of them budged, so Shirle took the initiative. She leaned in close and kissed him on the lips. He drew back at first because it was a little unexpected, but soon after he kissed her back and she accepted.

They went back and forth fumbling over each other, before they actually got the hang of things. Once they were on the same page, one thing lead to another all night until her roommate came home. They were both satisfied; they wouldn't have known the difference, because this was both of their first time.

A week later Shirle was packed up and headed to the State's never to see Timothy again, even though she wished they could be together. Once back at home she started to get very ill, no one knew what was going on. Naturally her parents thought that maybe she had brought something back with her from Asia, so they rushed her to the hospital. After several tests the doctors couldn't any foreign illness or anything else for that matter, until they ran a pregnancy test on her. The test result came back positive, and it was made right then and there that she would not have anything to do with that baby. Her mother tried to force her to have an abortion; however, her sister convinced her mother otherwise.

"Ma, let her have the baby, you know it's a sin to have an abortion. Let her have it and I'll raise it as it was mine." Her mother agreed and that's how her life turned out. Shirle saw her one time and that was in the delivery room, after that, her family sent her away again to a country overseas. They had gotten her some type of high paying, top clearance, secret service job. From that day forth, she would never speak of her child, nor would she ever see her again.

Her sister on the other hand was living the lavish life back at home, taking care of a child that their parents were basically paying her to take for. From the moment of birth, Tina was brought up into a lie. Her entire existence up until college was a lie, but at the same time, it was all she ever knew. She had the best of everything, wore the finest clothes, and attended the best schools. She was very privileged to say the least. She had everything handed to her from birth, and she knew how to keep it that way.

IVYON

Ivyon could not believe the events that transpired over the last few weeks, everything just happened so fast and out of nowhere, that it just seemed so unbelievable. First running into Vici after purposely avoiding her for an entire year, to running into Rufus and Josh within the same night; oh and what a night it turned out to be. Out of all other things, having sex with Vici again knowing damn well she shouldn't have, especially after hearing Vici's confession to her while assuming Ivyon was sound asleep the last sexual episode they had. Now this crazy bitch, Tina, broke onto her house pretending to be Vici in an effort to get between her legs, and boy did it work.

Talking to no one in particular, Ivyon said "I cannot believe this, this past month has just been crazy as hell. I just can't seem to catch a break, and through it all, I do not want to be alone. Who can I call? I know I'm not calling Vici; I can't keep doing that to her, I certainly can't call Rufus. I mean I could but I don't think I'm ready for all of that right now. My heart truly belongs to him and I would just melt right in his arms if I called him over. Maybe I should just call Tessia or Bronte just to talk!" Shaking her head, Ivyon was just in complete shock and confusion, she had no idea what was happening to her or why. She was under the impression that everything was ok for the past year, now it seemed as if the weight of the world would come crashing down on her shoulders. Not having a clue as to what to do next, Ivyon took a hot bath accompanied by a few cocktails to smooth her over and just simply called it a night, seeing how she was unable to come to any conclusion or resolution.

The next morning, Ivyon awoke to sunshine and what seemed to be a clear head. After making herself an omelet and a fresh squeezed glass of orange juice, she figured she'd do a little retail therapy on her own. What better way to clear your mind than to treat yourself to a few new things? Her first trip was to Pentagon City Mall in Arlington, VA. Not finding too much of anything there, Ivyon decided to take a drive down to Tyson's Corner Center. Being as though that was her favorite mall, she knew she could never go wrong. She needed for nothing, judging by all the clothes that occupied her closet with the tags still on them; however, a girl could never have too much. Ivyon went from store to store buying whatever her heart desired. After making a few trips to the parking garage to put her bags away, she realized she had been so caught up shopping; she hadn't even eaten anything since she left the house. Taking a break to get a bite to eat from the food court, Ivyon noticed that she had already spent 3 hours in that mall. Not having a care in the world, and taking some time to herself, Ivyon decided once she finished eating she'd continue her shopping.

Eating her lunch alone, occupied by just her thoughts, Ivyon caught a glimpse of someone starring at her from across the court. She smiled to herself before finishing her lunch and carrying on with her day. Macy's was next on her list of stores to flourish. She needed or wanted rather a new Dooney and Burke bag, Issey Miyake Floral and Coach Poppy perfumes. She made her way over to the bags and immediately fell in love. Narrowing her choice down to four, she couldn't decide which one she loved more, so naturally she grabbed them all. Walking toward the register to make her purchase, she saw the same guy from the food court following her around in Macy's. He was a very attractive young man, with muscular build, brown skin, slim with an extraordinary taste for casual clothes. His clothes fit his shape as if he was a mannequin and they were tailored made. Slim fit chocolate slacks, falling just right over his squared-toed caramel/chocolate Stacy Adam's, chocolate colored vest with a chocolate/caramel tie that lay over his caramel shirt, caramel leather band Breitling accented his wrist. Clearly this man had taste. There was no way in hell he was gonna try to kidnap her or cause her any harm, bad guys didn't down as casual as he had. Just the type of man she was into, reminding her of her dear love Rufus, and this man was definitely in her league. Ivyon turned her attention back to her objective walking toward the register, when she noticed that this fine specimen of a man was still behind her. She told the sales woman to hold her things, she needed to get something else. She made her way over to the lingerie section, locking eyes with her follower, making sure he was still in toe with her. She found a pink sheer number that she would be sure to try on. Looking over her shoulder to make sure he was still there, she smiled at him and made her way to the dressing room. She went to the dressing room and slipped out of her clothes and into the sexy number she picked up, once she had it on, she opened the door to see if her follower was still there. As she suspected, he was still there waiting for her to come out. She looked at him and smiled, gesturing with her index finger for him to join her. He looked around to make sure no one saw him and he quickly made his way to the dressing room to join her. Once inside the dressing room, he looked at her stunning body laced with this pink sheer one piece outfit, he licked his lips in an effort to speak before she put her finger to his mouth and said "shh". He looked over at her, wrapped his hands behind her head and kissed her deeply. Breaking loose from the kiss he licked a trail down her neck to her nipples and suckled them one by one making them as erect as pencil erasers. Ivyon was so deep in pleasure; she let her head drop back and let out a slight moan, letting him know that she was pleased.

Making his way back up to her neck, he reached around her, unzipping her one piece corset and slowly removing each strap from her shoulders, letting them drop one by one. Slowly revealing her caramel breasts and chocolate nipples, he cupped them both bringing them to his lips licking one nipple after the other. He slid her corset past her hips and over her feet, bringing her leg up over his shoulders; he teased her clit with his thumb before he could no longer resist devouring her flower. So much pleasure, Ivyon pulled at his clothes, holding on to the back of his head. Ivyon could not catch her breath from the attention this man was giving her, she held on tight to the back of his head hoping not to lose her balance. His tongue felt like a world wind, he would part her lips gently, make love to her tunnel with his tongue and then French kiss her clit. He pleased her undercarriage for all of 15 minutes straight, never coming up for air, experiencing her first orgasm, her knees buckled from under her. Never losing his rhythm, he caught her and stood her back up against the wall, this time putting both her legs around his shoulder's making sure she wouldn't lose her balance again. He continued to please her for the next 45 minutes, making sure every time he made her cum, he sucked her dry. Ivyon climaxed time after time; her body shook into convulsions. After this experience she was drained and exhausted. All she wanted to do now was curl up like a baby and go to sleep. Her mystery man finally came up for air and kissed her, allowing her to taste her essence on his lips. She went to say something to him and he stopped her with a finger to his lips, handing her his card, he whispered "you taste wonderful". With that he walked away leaving her in awe. Leaving her speechless, he made his way to the register where Ivyon left her things, handed the cashier his "Black Card" and told her to ring up

Ivyon's things. Ivyon sat in the dressing rooming, gathering her clothes and pulling herself together, she looked down at his card and noticed that he owned real estate across the country.

Ivyon could not believe her day. She had not planned for this, yet she loved every moment if it. It completely put her mind at ease and gave her great satisfaction. The thought ran across her mind that she hadn't gotten the chance to please him. After getting dressed she made her way to the counter, she handed the cashier her corset and her credit card, only to find out that her mystery man had already paid for her entire purchase. The cashier took the corset and asked "did you want to pay for this separately? The gentleman already paid for everything else." Ivyon looked at her with confusion and shook her head yes. All she could think was "what a day."

RUFUS

Throughout my life I've had many women. I come from a very wealthy family; I never wanted for anything, I don't even have to work now because my family's money is older than I am. However, unlike my sister and brother, I could not just allow myself to stay home and do nothing. I had dreams and goals that I sat out to accomplish. I wanted to make my own money so I would never have to depend on anyone. We went to all private schools and I worked hard to graduate top of my class all through my educational career. I made the Dean's List every semester, not something that occurs often with black kids.

That's just the thing, unlike many others I know, I refused to be a statistic or think I'm any better than anyone else just because I grew up fortunate. I may not have come up poor or know what it's like to have my parents struggle over ways to pay the mortgage or light bill; however, I dealt with my own struggle of trying to fit in with all the white kids I grew up with and went to school with. The other kid's always made me feel like we weren't worthy enough to go to the same schools as they did, so I made it a personal goal to graduate top of my class. I proved that not only was I worthy, but that I was better than anyone of them. I had to prove that I did not just get through off my family's money and name. I attended some of the finest schools to receive my education. I graduated top of my class from Harvard University receiving my Bachelor's and my Master's Degrees. I attended Johns Hopkins University to receive my Ph.D., did my residency and also to obtain my Doctoral Degree. I am a World Class Neuro Surgeon at Johns Hopkins Hospital in Baltimore, Maryland with a Ph.D. in Clinical Psychology.

I own and run my own Psychology Practice. I own my
home along with a beach home in Barbados and a vacation
villa in the South of France. Money has never been an issue
for me and there hasn't been anything out of my reach,
except my sweet Ivyon, who I long to be with every day.
Sex isn't an issue for me, but with her is where I want to
be. She is definitely a different breed of woman. I don't
care about her sexual escapades, I can cure all of that, and I
would take care of all her needs. All she needs is love,
understanding, compassion, and a sense of security and
trust. I can provide her with all of this and more, but I
betrayed her trust when I slept with that slut.

It all just happened so fast and out of nowhere. But now I
see it was all a plot to get back at the one I love because she
wouldn't love her. If I could take it all back, I would
without even a thought about it. Ivyon is my life and
without her there's nothing I need to live for. I have to
make her see that she's the only one for me, but I also have
to give her some time and space to make up her mind, I just
hope she's quick with it and comes back to me.

All these things and more ran through Rufus' mind as he
sat and tried to think of a way he could get Ivyon back. He
wanted nothing more in life.

I'll send her something to speed up the process and
hopefully she'll take the bait and realize I really am sorry.

I can't believe I was so stupid to have cheated on Ivy, she
was in so much pain, all she needed for me to be there for
her, and I betrayed her. It's no shock that she turned away
from me in the club. I have to do something to get her back;

she is my heart and my soul. Without her I'm nothing. Rufus thought to himself as he desperately tried to come up with a plan to get her back.

The roses didn't work the last time, but who's to say that won't work this time? Ivyon loves roses, so I'll just send her more. Rufus called the florist and arranged to have two dozen each of red, white, pink and yellow roses delivered. He also sent her an edible arrangement along with a dozen chocolate covered strawberries. Rufus was determined to win his girl back. There was no more in heart or life for anyone else, he just wanted Ivyon.

Rufus felt like he was fighting a losing battle trying to get Ivyon back. He understood that he was wrong as two left shoes, but the situation was not in his control. Yes he was man enough to have fought Tina off, but what guy would. Because he didn't, that would be his down fall. He would have to live with the fact that he just might lose Ivyon altogether. Rufus didn't want to accept that chance so he would fight until the end.

~~~*~~~

Ivyon had a buzz at her front gate; she went to the monitoring system to see who it might be because she wasn't expecting anyone. To her surprise, there was a florist and edible arrangement truck at her gate trying to get in. She let them through and when she opened her front door, the assortment of roses was astonishing, she couldn't believe her eyes. They were accompanied by an edible arrangement big enough for an office party to feast on and a box of two dozen white and milk chocolate covered strawberries.

Ivyon smiled so big she tried to hide it behind her hands. There was a note attached to each dozen of roses, and each one read the same thing "I'M SORRY". Ivyon could not believe her eyes; finally she reached the note attached to the strawberries,

"Ivy, I know I messed up and there's nothing I can say that would change what I did. I need you to know that my intensions were never to hurt you. I love you with every breath I take, and life without you is miserable. I will never stop trying to win you back and prove to you that I am the only person you'll ever need in your life to make you whole. I love you Ivy, please come back to me. Love, Rufus"

That made Ivyon's heart melt, she cried right there on the porch. If this is what love felt like, she wanted to be wrapped in it every day of her life. Still being precautious, she had to protect her heart. She realized that she was maybe being a little selfish, she knew Rufus could never intentionally do something like this to her, she just didn't want to risk getting hurt again.

~~~*~~~

Rufus went on to work being optimistic that his plan worked. Even if it didn't, it felt good to know that he at least tried. He would continue to try until Ivyon came back to him with opened arms. He didn't care the cost, because you couldn't place a price tag on Ivyon. She was everything, she was exceptional, extraordinary, lovable, sweet, passionate, kind, and trustworthy, she was everything a man could want in a woman. She was the true definition of beautiful; he worshiped the ground she walked on.

Ivyon had her own successful business, she owned her house and a private beach house, she owned her cars, and she could take care of herself. She was a woman with much class; she was truly a force to be reckoned with. She demanded respect and everyone gave it to her. She just had that way about her; she was sexy in every aspect of the word.

IVYON

I have to call Vici and let her know about Tina's crazy ass.

Ivyon called Vici and told her everything that happened; even that Rufus sent her roses and candy. Vici wanted to come over so she could talk face to face with Ivy about the situation, also in hopes that Ivyon would let her console her. Considering Vici's true feelings for Ivyon, she quickly dismissed Vici's offer. For her own selfish reasons, Ivyon did want Vici there, to hold her, to kiss her, to caress her; however, Ivyon had a deeper love in her heart for Vici and their friendship. Ivyon just didn't want to risk compromising that over sex. Through it all Vici has always been there for Ivyon. Ivyon needed her more as a friend, especially if things ultimately didn't go right between her and Rufus. In the mist of everything happening, Ivyon hadn't spent much time with Derek, not even to talk to him. This just was not like her; she would have to give Derek a call.

"Hey Sunshine, I haven't talked to you in almost a month. Is everything okay?"

"Yes dad, everything's fine, I've just been a little busy. How are things with you?"

"Things are wonderful. I just got a contract for a building in Dubai and I was wondering if we could go in together on it and become business partners? We would split everything right down the middle. I know how you love your vacations when you go over there, so I went ahead and bought the property as a gift to you. I have a lot of business ventures out there, so this just seemed to be the perfect plan for us both. What do you think?"

"That's great dad."

"That's it? Something must be wrong. Usually you would be ecstatic to hear anything about Dubai. Tell me what's going on?"

"Nothing's going on, I'm fine dad."

"Ivyon, I'm your father, and even though I've missed out on the first 21-22 years of your life, I know now when something's bothering you. You know there's nothing you have to hold back from me, tell me what's wrong?"

"I know dad, I just didn't want to bother you with my crazy life. This is something I have to deal with."

"Ivy, either you tell me now or I'll be on the next flight out there. You know I'll do it so spill it."

"Okay dad. Pour yourself a Scotch and have a seat." Ivyon began telling her father everything about how Vici confessed about her love for Ivyon while she was under the impression that she was asleep. To how Tina broke into her home and sexually assaulted her, portraying to be Vici. She told him how desperately she wanted to be back with Rufus.

"Wow Ivy, I'm sorry you are going through this. You should get a restraining order against Tina or have her arrested. Vici doesn't know that you heard her confession so I wouldn't tell her; however, I would stop the sexual relationship, just to create boundaries and you're not leading her on. As far as Rufus goes, I know he messed up and I understand you're hurt and your stand point on this; however, he apologized and I know that does not make it right, but he also was tricked into it. I know that doesn't justify it or make it right. Do you honestly believe in your heart that he would have cheated on you under normal circumstances? If not, I think you should take him back, but not without giving yourself time to heal and recover and not without rules. You have to let him know what's acceptable and what's not, and let him know how he really made you feel."

"I'm not saying that you have to rush back into things with him Ivy. Take it slow, actually date him this time. When's the last time you've been on an actual date? Let him court you. Have him come to your house to pick you up, when he arrives he should ring your bell, flowers in hand, greet you with a kiss on your hand and escort you to his car. He should open the door for you and make sure you're comfortable before getting in the car. He should take you to the finest restaurant, where you eat the finest foods and drink the finest wines, all while he waits on you to start off the conversation with whatever is weighing heavy on your heart and mind. He should treat you no less than the Queen you are."

"Dad, you always know what to say, thank you for the advice and most of all listening without a biased or judgmental ear."

"You don't have to thank me. You're my daughter and I'm always going to have you best interest at heart. Now if you really want to thank me, you can do so my taking me up on my offer. I haven't seen you in a while and I know how much you love to vacation there, so you can make it out to be a vacation with your friends."

"Dad, this is our trip, something you've gone through the trouble and did for me, so I wouldn't feel right taking anybody along."

"Nonsense, you and your friends go on down there and enjoy yourselves and maybe your last day or two I'll come down so we can look over the property and discuss some things and you can finish off your vacation."

"Dad that's really wonderful, thank you."

"You're very welcome. If you don't mind me asking, who will you take with you?"

"Well Vic is my only true friend…"

"Now Ivy, think about what we just discussed, maybe you should include your sister or Tessia. I bet Tessia could use a vacation. I wouldn't mind enjoying one with her."

"Hey now, you stay away from her, you're married."
Ivyon said while laughing. Her dad was always a little fresh on Tessia since Ivyon first introduced them. Ivyon thought they would make a good couple; only thing was that they both were married. Derek more so than Tessia, seeing as how Jordan was incarcerated at the time for raping Ivyon. But Derek was actively still married.

"Maybe I will take all of them. What better way to enjoy a vacation than with all my girls."

"Okay Pumpkin, you let me know when and I'll set up the meeting time. Love you, call me later."

"I love you too Dad."

Wow my dad sure knows how to bring my spirits up. He was so right about everything, even down to cutting out my sex life with Vici. Ugh, I'm going to hate to do that especially since I'm not getting it from nowhere else. Well I guess I better call up the girls to see when they will be available to go on a two week vacation.

Ivyon made all of her appropriate calls and arrangements to have her trip set up. She planned to leave within the next two weeks and vacation there for two weeks at least. She definitely needed some time to relax and let go. Now the only thing left for her to do was to call Rufus to thank him for the arrangements.

"Hello!"

"Well hello there Mr. Doctor."

"Ivy?"

"Who else would it be calling you that?"

"No one, I was just in shock. How are you?"

"I'm fine. How about yourself?"

"Now that I've heard your voice, my world has gotten a little bit brighter."

"You are too smooth Rufus. I just called to thank you for the flowers, fruit and candy. I really loved them, and you know roses are my favorite."

"You don't have to thank me, those things are just a portion of my love for you, but I could give you so much more. You never have to want for anything Ivy. I'm so sorry for hurting you and I know it's going to take more than an apology, but I just want you to know that I never meant to hurt you and I am not whole without you."

"Slow down Rufus. I believe you love me and that you never meant to hurt me, but you did. I put my all into you and I'm still hurt behind it. It's going to take more than candy and flowers to get me to trust you again."

"I understand and I'm willing to do whatever it is that you need me to do Ivy, I just want you back. Let me take you to dinner for starters, I want to see your bright eyes and smile, your radiant glow, and smell your sweet scent. Will you have dinner with me?"

VICI

Even though what happened to Ivyon was tragic, hurtful, and terrifying, the way that she spoke about how Tina handled her, made Vici tremble inside. Not due to fear, but due to the amount of ecstasy she received from the story. Vici had to get some type of satisfaction now, whether she pleased herself, called Byran and let him tease the inside of her tunnel or if she called one of her many, many girlfriends. The one person that she knew for sure could do the trick, she wouldn't dare to ask her after already going through so much, all she could do right now was be there for Ivyon in her time of need. But of course, if Ivyon needed her in a special way, Vici was sure to be there with bells and whistles on.

Vici decided to call a longtime friend of hers whom she hadn't really dealt with in years; she decided to call Payton. Payton was fair skinned, with sandy brown, curly hair and hazel eyes. She was about 5' 7" with a slim build. Payton looked like a model. She could have been a Victoria's Secret model had she not gotten caught up in Michael, she had a contract with them and everything. Men sure do know how to pull the wool over our eyes and make us forget about everything. Payton had the perfect body from head to toe, she wore a size 7 show, 32 inch waist line, 36C cup size and the ass was just right. She had the sweetest taste and smell to her, no one could deny this woman even if they wanted to. She would bring men to their knees and women to her feet. Payton was deadly, like Vici, she knew both sides of the fence; however, she knew them better. She ultimately turned Vici out. Vici was Payton's project, she taught her everything she knew. Payton had Vici eating out the palms of her hands if and/or whenever Payton called.

Vici would drop everything for her. It was so bad, Vici found herself failing classes because of this woman. That was a situation Vici had to soon get herself out of before she reached the point of no return. Vici knew that revisiting her past would probably hurt her, but she needed to mix things up a bit. She wanted a taste of the dark side, she wanted Payton.

"Hey Payton, it's Vici. How have you been?"

"Vici? My sweet, timid little Vici? I've been good. How about you?"

"I've been well."

"So Vici, what do I owe the pleasure of this call?"

"Uhm, well I have some things I wanted to talk to you about and I was wondering if you had any time this afternoon or evening that you could spare to meet up with me?"

"Hmm, I don't think I would have time today, this is such short notice. Well what did you want to discuss?"

"Just some new business ideas I wanted your opinion on. I was thinking about doing something in fashion and I know you're the perfect person to talk to about that type of stuff."

"Oh, okay. Well I'm honored that you had me in mind. What are you doing tomorrow?"

"So far, nothing. I'm going down to the barber shop today around 6 for a fresh cut. I like to be the last person so I don't have a long wait time. So tomorrow I'm free pretty much all day."

"Fresh cut? So you still wear a short cut, huh?"

"Yeah, pretty much, it's so much easier to deal with. I just wake up in the morning and I'm ready to go. I don't even have to brush it, it's so close."

"Well okay, give me a call in the morning and we'll set something up."

"Okay, well it was nice talking to you."

"Okay, look forward to talking to you tomorrow."

Vici was a little disappointed that her plan didn't really pan out. She would just have to wait until tomorrow. Vici went on ahead with her plans for the day, making market, exercising and finally going to the barber shop.

"Hey Tony, can I get the usual today?"

"Hey Vici. Yeah, you know I got you."

"Cool. How long do I have to wait?"

"Uh. I should be done in about 15 minutes, just have to finish up his shape up and close up the shop and I'll be ready for you."

"Okay well I'll just hang out here, no rush."
Vici sat in the waiting area, reading a month-old copy of Hip Hop Magazine, something she wasn't interested in. She really didn't even take the time out to read, just flipped through the pages waiting on Tony to finish up. She stopped on an article about Christ Brown when she heard Tony call out to her.

"Hey Vici you can take a seat in my chair. I'm going to lock up the shop and I'll be right back."
Vici placed the magazine back on the table and started walking toward the back. Before sitting in the chair, Vici removed all her clothing except for her bra. Not only did Vici get her head shaved, but her kitten, too. She liked to be well manicured down below, so she always paid Tony extra for the cut with a straight razor. It was well worth the extra pay, because after he shaved her bald, she was in for a special treat. Vici heard from a distance the door close and Tony turned the lock. He was walking toward her when he heard someone bang on the door. They looked at each other wondering who that could be. Vici grabbed a cape and covered herself while Tony went to see who was at the door.

"Hi, can I help you?"

"Yes. I needed a shape-up really quick."

"Oh, I'm sorry ma'am, but we just closed up for the evening."

"Come on please, just really quick. A friend of mine guaranteed me that I could come here and receive excellent service."

"Oh yeah? What might your friend's name be?"

"You may know her by Vici."

"Oh really? Vici, I do know her, as a matter of fact, she's here now about to get some work done. Well since you're a a good friend of hers. I'll do you before I start her."

"Oh, thank you so much this means a lot to me, but you don't have to take me first, she was here before me."

"Well she has some special work that I have to do. Trust me, she won't mind."

"Okay, if you insist."

As they walked toward the back, Vici was surprised to see Payton there. She couldn't believe her eyes. Payton didn't wear a short cut and she didn't tell Vici that she would be there this evening, she told her that she was busy. When Payton laid eyes on Vici, a smile came to both their faces. Vici jumped up half naked to greet Payton, losing her cape in the process. Payton caught a glimpse and was pleased at what she saw.

"Wow, what did I walk into here?"

"Oh this is nothing; Tony shaves me down under closer than I get with his straight razor."

"Really? I was thinking about doing the same thing, but I couldn't find anyone that I trusted enough. Do you mind if I admire the work in progress?"

"No, not at all. Tony do you mind?'

"Hey, it's your piece that's going to be exposed. If it's okay with you, then it's okay with me."

"Okay, cool."

Vici sat back down in her seat, cocked her legs open and propped them up on the arm rest. Allowing Tony full access and providing Payton with an Eagles eye view.

Payton sat back silently as she watched Tony lather up Vici's secret box. Payton watched as Tony dipped his shaving brush into the shaving cream and slowly applied it to Vici; he made sure that he handled her with care. He stayed within the lines, making sure not to get any on her inner thighs. Breaking Payton out of her trance, she heard Vici talking to her.

"Payton what brings you down here, I thought you were busy today?

"Well I was at first, but then I remembered that I needed a shape up also, and I thought about you. So I figured that I could come down with you."

"A shape up? Your hair is damn near in the middle of your back. What are you up to Payton?"
Payton smiled an innocent smile, she walked over toward Vici, leaned down and planted a soft kiss on her lips and said, "after thinking about it, I had to see you."
Tony peaked his head from between Vici's legs with a look of surprise on his face. He looked at both women and quickly but his head back down. After Payton kissed her, Vici was speechless, so Payton kissed her again. This Vici accepted and willingly gave Payton tongue. The women locked in a tango with their tongues while Tony sat and watched, growing stiffer and stiffer within his pants, unable to contain his erection. Vici pushed her chest forward and let out a sigh of relief; Tony quickly finished his work and wiped away any remainder with a damp, warm towel. He sat back and watched while the ladies engaged in what seemed to be a hot and passionate kiss. They were locked in on each other as if they were long time lover's separated by time and brought back together by a whisper on a drifty breeze. After about two minutes of passionate kissing, Tony noticed Payton's hands starting to travel toward

Vici's breast. After she found them, she traced circles around Vici's nipples right before she vigorously cupped her breast. Vici leaned back and moaned as she received pleasure from Payton. Tony could no longer hold his composure after watching the lustfulness take place in front of him He dropped his head between Vici's legs and began tracing her inner lips with his tongue. Up and down, up and down, crossing over to her bud and suckling on it before traveling down to her tunnel, poking it in and out. Repeating all these motions, up and down, in and out, slowly pushing Vici to ecstasy. Payton stopped kissing Vici and started kissing her breast. Vici was in Heaven receiving so much pleasure. This is exactly what she needed to take the edge off; to get her to where she needed to be.

Tony and Payton took turns French kissing all the important parts on Vici and she let them; however, she wanted to join in the fun. She told Payton to take her clothes off and for Tony to sit her on Vici's face. They both did as they were instructed. Once on top of her face, Payton spread her legs to the 3 and 9 position, braced herself on the shoulder rest of Vici's chair and bounced up and down on Vici's stiff tongue. After reaching an orgasm on Vici's tongue, Payton dropped herself down, lay on top of Vici, spread her legs and told Tony to taste them both. Tony had himself a smorgasbord of flavors, giving both ladies the pleasure they needed, wanted, and deserved, while he fucked them both with his tongue, he massaged the shaft of his penis causing a bit of pre-cum to drop from the head. Payton climbed down from off Vici and dropped to her knees, she took Tony fully into her mouth while she inserted her finger in Vici's ass. Vici was the main attraction of tonight's show, she was to receive all the pleasure, and so she did.

Shortly after, the women switched places. Vici giving Tony some head while he tasted Payton spread Eagle style in the chair. Vici teased the head of Tony's soldier for quite a bit, bringing him to near eruption, before she would stop and let him catch his breath. Payton got up from the chair and grabbed her bag. What she pulled out made Vici's cheeks flush. A 10 inch pink strap on; Payton suited up with the strap on, lubed it down and told Tony to get in the chair. After he did so, she instructed Vici to ride him while she rode Vici from behind. Both Vici's holes were filled and she did not object. Vici rode both dicks as if they were trying to run away. After causing Tony to climax, Vici pulled Payton in front of her, lay her on Tony's check while she ate her until she climaxed. After bringing Payton to her orgasm, Vici turned around in the 69 position allowing Payton to fuck her hard from behind on top of Tony while she got him hard again with her mouth. There was so much pleasure being given and received within that one chair. Once Vici reached her climax, she worked the shaft on Tony's dick like she was starting a fire to bring him to another orgasm.

This triangle of love went on for hours until no one literally could stand anymore, they all passed out in the middle of the floor. Panting hard, chest raising and falling trying to catch their breaths, they all lay together in a pile in the middle of the floor and went to sleep.

BRONTE

Wow, Ivy planned this wonderful trip and I have nothing to take with me. Sounds like a shopping spree to me. So much to do in so little time."

Bronte had all sorts of thoughts running through her mind. So excited about the trip, she forgot all about Ivyon's sexual assault. She felt helpless because she couldn't help Ivyon. She didn't know who the assailant was or anything, all she knew was this chick whoever she was had an infatuation with her sister and she wanted her bad. Realizing she had so much to do before the trip gave her an instant headache, she felt in the mood for a little R&R. With no stable or steady man in her life made it a little harder to get some R&R. One person she knew for sure that could satisfy her needs, she hasn't heard from lately. Bronte decided to give her a call.

"Hey Sweetie."

"Hi, how are you?"

"I'll be doing much better if I could see you. I haven't heard from you lately, is everything okay?"

"Oh yeah, everything's fine. I've just been a little sick; I didn't want to get you sick. But I'm fine now.

"Oh okay. Well that was thoughtful. Are you busy this evening? I was thinking we could have dinner, or maybe we could be dinner. I could come over and heal you with my touch, or should I say my tongue?"

Tina had to think of something fast. She didn't want to push Bronte away to make anything suspicious; she needed her to get close to Ivyon. However, she couldn't allow Bronte to come over anymore because her obsession had grown for Ivyon. She now had a mural of Ivyon painted on her bedroom wall. The image was of Ivyon in all white, standing facing the wing, forcing her hair to blow away from her face; absolutely breathtaking. Tina stole that picture from Bronte's album one night while Bronte was asleep. One day after looking through her album showing off some pictures to Tina, Bronte noticed the picture was missing. Bronte and Tina both looked all around Bronte's house for it. Tina knew they would never find it because she had it.

"Uhm, I would love that, but there's just one thing. I decided to paint and rearrange my house so it's kind of a mess. How about I just come to your house? I haven't been there in a while, and you wouldn't have to worry about getting dressed or anything."

"Well that's sweet. What time do you think you'll be here? I can't wait to see you."

"Well I have to shower and get dressed, so maybe in about 2 hours. That's including that one hour travel time. I enjoy coming to see you, but have you ever considered moving closer? I mean you're out there all alone."

"Why would I move closer? The only family that I have is Ivyon and she lives in PA."

"You wouldn't want to be closer to her? I mean you guys are close right, what if she had an emergency, how would you get to her?"

"Well, I've never really thought about it. Come to think of it, she did have an emergency about 2 weeks ago. Some woman broke into her house and sexually assaulted her. She thought it was her friend."

"Really? Wow is she okay?"

"Yeah she's fine, my sister is strong, she can get through anything."

"Well does she know who it was? Did she call the cops or anything?"

"Yes, she knows who it was. She said it was some girl named Tina that's obsessed with her. I mean this girl is really crazy. This isn't the first time she's done something to my sister. I wish I knew who it was, I'd hurt her for hurting my sister. But anyway, she didn't call the cops; she said that she tried to shoot her while she was climbing over the gate."

"Wow that is crazy. Some people just really need some help."

"Yeah, but anyway, I should see you in about two hours or should?"

"Yes sweetie, I'll be there."

Bronte was happy now. She was about to get some much needed sexual pleasure. Something her body was yearning for. She'd figured she'd get her release, relax for the rest of the evening. In the morning she would go to work and go down to the National Harbor on her lunch break to do a little shopping for the trip.

Bronte had no idea that she was being deceived and lied to by this woman whom she had thought had a genuine interest in her. All she knew was this woman made her feel things she's never felt before and she loved every minute of it.

TINA

Well now I know that Ivyon hasn't called the police and Bronte still doesn't suspect anything or know about me. That's ultimately a good thing; I don't want her to know anything. I need her as bait to get to my most prized possession. Ivyon loves me; she just doesn't know it yet. I just have to come up with a way to get her to trust me so I can show her how much I love her and what she's missing every moment she spends away from me. I have to think of something, come up with some kind of plan.

Tina put her fingers up to her nose as if she could still smell Ivyon's scent on them, all the while staring at her painting.

"Uhm…you smell and taste so sweet, all I can think about is you. When I taste your sister, I imagine it's you. When I run my fingers through her hair, I imagine it's you. When I caress her skin, I imagine it's you. When she screams out my name, I imagine it's you. I've had the pleasure of making you cum on my tongue and now I want more.

I imagine us happy together, in our own world. No one to come in between us, I can have you all to myself. I thought I got rid of that pasty doctor, but I can see that he's determined. I'll have to remove him from the picture permanently. Bronte doesn't suspect anything yet, but I won't hesitate to get rid of your sister too if she tries to get in our way."

Tina sat at the edge of her bed on her padded chest talking to Ivyon as if she was really there. She threw her legs up and continued to stare into Ivyon's eyes wishing they were together. She took two fingers and sucked on them before inserting them into her already dripping wet vagina. She massaged her breast with her right hand while she masturbated to the thought of Ivyon. Shivering from a massive orgasm, she climaxed at least three times before reaching satisfaction. Now she had to go and bring Bronte to her climax. She never let Bronte down in that department because she always envisioned it was Ivyon that she was pleasing.

While she drove to Bronte's house, she thought of a way she could taste Ivyon again.

"Maybe I could ask Bronte to bring her into one of our sexual escapades. I don't know Bronte may have a problem with that since that's her sister. Damn, I have to think of something."

Once Tina reached Bronte's house, there was no time to talk, she wanted to have her, she had Ivyon heavy on her mind and this excited her in a sexual way. Soon as Bronte answered the door, Tina stepped inside, cuffed the back of Bronte's neck and kissed her passionately, causing Bronte to stumble and try to catch her breath once she released her. Bronte put her hand to her mouth and looked at Tina, immediately Bronte reached for her and kissed her with the same amount of passion, all the while taking off Tina's blouse. They stood there in the front hallway kissing each other passionately and recklessly tearing each other's clothes off.

Tina pulls Bronte into the kitchen pushing her up against the counter, cuffing her breast and stuffing them in her mouth. She forcefully turns Bronte around and brings her hand around the front of Bronte's body and she starts massaging her clit. Bronte enjoys every moment of this unexpected sexual chemistry, it turned her on to new heights. Her legs began to shake as she goes into convulsions, she can barely stand so she let her body fall on top of the counter. This aroused Tina more forcing her to up her standards on the amount of pleasure she gave.

She swung Bronte around in a fit of passionate rage, she picked her up and placed her on top of the counter, pushing her body back and pulling her legs forward, Tina dove into Bronte's valley as if she was never going to eat again. Bronte received so much sexual intensity and pleasure, when she climaxed, she came really hard.

Nothing and no one could match the sex between Bronte and Tina; and Bronte knew it. From the kitchen they moved to the bedroom where Tina put on her strap-on to continue Bronte's multiple orgasms. This was by far the best night of Bronte's sexual life. After being pleased for all of two hours, Bronte was exhausted, Tina cradled her in her arm's something she never does, all the while trying to devise a plan.

"Not to sound ungrateful Tina but you've never stayed this long before, let alone held me. Is everything alright?"

"Sure honey, everything's fine. You know they say, all good things come with time."

Bronte was shocked so she just lay there and took it all in. She didn't know what was going on she just knew she liked it.

"I see you have suitcases out, you plan on going somewhere?"

"Oh yeah, my sister planned this two week vacation to Dubai. She loves it there, she goes maybe twice a year and this time she planned it for about four of us to go and lay in the sun."

"Oh wow, that sounds wonderful. You said she was assaulted right, how is she recovering?"

"I think she's doing pretty good, I mean she has to be for her to plan this trip."

"I think we should do something nice for her."

"Wow, what's up with the sudden interest in my sister?"

"Nothing, she just seems like she's been through a lot and maybe she needs something to take her mind off things."

"Maybe you're right. What did you have in mind?"

"Well I guess that depends on what she likes to do."
Laughing Bronte said,
"The only thing I know she really likes to do is have sex."

That was all Tina needed to hear in order to come up with a plan.

"Really, is she into women? I mean if you don't mind, I could ease her mind for her."

Bronte looked at Tina like she was crazy and said, "I don't know. I don't impose on her sex life like that. I don't know if I would want the woman I'm sleeping with to have sex with my sister. Let's just leave it alone, this trip will do her justice."

Temporarily defeated, Tina left it alone for now….

RUFUS

Ivyon is finally giving me another chance to prove myself;
I have to do this right. I'll send my limo to pick her up,
making sure he arrives at 6:30 p.m. I'll make sure that I
stock the limo with Chardonnay for her and two dozen long
stem red and white roses. She love's Luther Vandross so
I'll make sure that she's serenated with his voice.

I've already made reservations to rent out the roof top of
her restaurant "La'Moora', I know once her manager tells
her the details of how much I paid, she won't be upset. I
had them place bouquets of roses and lilac's accompanied
by candle light for good measure. Her master chef has been
rented out to me also so I know there won't be any
disappointments in her dish. Everything should be all set
for the wonderful evening. Whatever I have to do to win
over my girl, I will.

Ivyon was sitting in her living room around 6:30 p.m.
wondering if she'd made the right decision. She knew in
her heart that she wanted to be with this man and that she
was in love with him. There was no doubt in her mind that
he was in love with her also. She just didn't want to get
hurt again.

Suddenly the intercom rang and brought Ivyon out of her
thoughts. Ivyon went over to the panel to see who it was.
Noticing the limo, she buzzed him in. By the time she
reached her front door she was met by a well-dressed driver
who took her hand and escorted her to the car. He opened
her door for her and watched as she got into the car, once
inside; he raced around the other side and got in.

Ivyon was delighted at the sight in front of her. She picked up her glass of wine, took a sip and took in the aroma of the flowers and allowed the sound of Luther rock her into relaxation. Once they arrived at La'Moora' she was a little bit confused, she just assumed that Rufus would bring her back to his place, but Rufus obviously had different plans. Rufus greeted her at the kitchen door of her own restaurant, bending at the waist and taking her hand to his lips, he kissed it gently.

Ivyon wasn't surprised, that was just the type of gentleman that Rufus was. He took her by the hand and guided her upstairs to the roof top dining area, where she was greeted with dozens of assorted bouquets, while soft music penetrated her ears and the candle light complimented her skin. Once at the table, the already poured, chilled Chardonnay awaited her while her Master Chef, Mr. Charles waited patiently to take her order. Once she made her decision, Mr. Charles walked away to prepare their meal, Ivyon looked over at Rufus and smiled. Rufus smiled and automatically gratefully accepted his stamp of approval.

  "Ivyon, I cannot tell you enough how sorry I am. I know that's not enough but whatever you want me to do, I will. I know words really don't mean anything but my actions will prove that without you I am no longer in existence. I never meant to hurt you. What I did was completely wrong and unspeakable. I'm not trying to justify it; I just want you to know that I am really sorry."

Ivyon looked at Rufus with tears welled up in her eyes. She closed her eyes and the water works flowed; she put her head down and wiped the tears away. She tried to stop crying but every time she looked at him, the tears would start again.

"Rufus, I need you to understand that I'm not your normal girl, which means I hurt differently. You have no idea what I come from and how I survived. Before you, there was only one other main boyfriend in my life. When he hurt me, I was just graduating high school. I never forgave him because just like this situation, I never gave him a reason to betray my trust. I thought everything between us was wonderful, we never had any problems, he was technically my first, and just like you, he had to have his cake and eat it too. I come from a life time of pain and I don't want to and shouldn't have to hurt anymore."

Rufus never uttered a word while she spoke. He sat there patiently and quietly because he knew he was wrong and he could feel her hurt. Ivyon sat there with tear drenched cheeks; blood shot eyes, and was desperately trying to get him to understand her and to love her, to take her with open arms. Rufus reached across the table and wiped her tears away.

"Ivy, tell me what happened to you. Tell me all the things you've been keeping from me. Tell me who has hurt you and let me wipe your pain away. Tell me why you're so guarded and afraid. Tell me your deepest secrets. Tell me what makes you hurt, what makes you cry, so I'll know to never do those things and I can shelter you from them. I love you unconditionally, I cannot pass judgment on you and I will not make you feel ashamed. I want you to know that I love you, all of you no matter what has happened to you or what you've done."

Ivyon was relieved to know that he still had a serious interest in her no matter what.

"Rufus, I'm going on vacation for two weeks to Dubai to clear my head and handle some business with my dad. If you're really interested in who I am and what's happened to me, then I'll tell you when I return. Let's not waste this beautiful evening."

"Okay."

Rufus took that and left it alone for now. He was determined to know everything about her and all her hurt; however, he would just have to wait until she came back. He planned to shower her with as much love, attention, and devotion that she would allow him to.

He felt as though Ivyon was his reason for existence, so he made it a point to do whatever he could to keep her within his grasp. True love conquered all and he was definitely in love with Ms. Ivyon Moore.

VICI

Vici was ecstatic that Ivyon planned a trip for them to Dubai. She wasn't so happy about the fact that Ivyon ultimately chose Rufus. Although it was inevitable, she knew it was coming, she just hoped in her heart that she would choose her.

Ivyon called and told Vici all the details about her date with Rufus and how she planned to tell him about her life. Vici in turn was happy for Ivyon because she was happy; Vici would never want anything less than the best for Ivyon. Even though Vici had a deep love for Ivyon that without comparison, she knew that Ivyon held that same love for Rufus. Vici realized that she should have made her move for Ivyon back when they were in college; however, she knew that Ivyon had been hurt beyond repair at that point and so she needed to find herself. Now Vici was stuck wondering if she'd let Ivyon take too much time to find herself.

Vici has now come to the realization that now is the time to move in and start dating, obviously she'd lost Ivyon but she will remain hopeful in getting her back. A little distraught and heart broken, Vici went under the radar until the day before their trip. She had to get as much sex as possible in order to keep her mind off Ivyon in a sexual way during their trip together.

Vici thought that having sex with someone else would fill the void in her heart for Ivyon. She called Bryan, her friend she had met the night she took Ivyon to the club to try and get her back in the dating game. Vici spent 10 days in the presence of this man. No explanation as to what they were doing, no heads up as to her spending so much time with him or anything. He didn't seem to mind; actually he was grateful for all the passionate, rough, hardcore, unadulterated sex he could handle. Vici made angry love to this man as if he was truly Ivyon.

One night after a hard day's work, Bryan entered the front door and Vici jumped on him and kissed him forcefully; stopping just long enough to tear his clothes off him. Enjoying the roughness, Bryan spun around slamming Vici's back against the wall while biting on her neck. He unzipped his pants and roughly jammed his penis inside Vici in one swift movement, giving her exactly what she was looking for. Vici arched her back against the door to better support herself as she thrust her pelvis against Bryan's. They met each other's thrust with the same amount of passion.

Ultimately Vici tried to release all her hurt and pain into the sex they were having. Bryan in turn loved every moment of it and didn't want it to end. He started falling for her. He was interested from the moment they met, but Vici made it obvious that she didn't want to be in a relationship, but yet here she was with him without any explanation.

Bryan noticed something different about Vici, she was always distant, but now she was there every day for the past nine days straight, having sex with him as if it was the end of the world. From a man's stand point, unlimited, no boundaries sex was a dream, but at the same time, he wanted this woman. Bryan thought he would talk to her and see if she now wanted to be in a relationship with him.

"Vici, I was thinking that maybe we should consider being together."

Vici looked shocked at first, never really thinking about the outcome or his feelings for that matter. She was there for her own selfish reasons.

"Being together? What's wrong with what we're doing?"

"Well nothing's wrong with it. You don't want more?"

"I thought this was the dream of all men. Having as much sex as they wanted without having to be committed?"

"For most men who aren't looking for anything more. But I'm almost 35 years old and I want more. Sleeping around is not going to do it anymore for me. Having you here every night when I go to sleep and waking up to you every morning is something I could get used to, it is a really good feeling."

"Wow, I never looked at it as such. I didn't realize you had feelings for me or that you wanted more than this?"

"Vici, you are a wonderful woman. You're gorgeous, you have a magnetic personality, and you're sweet, loving and caring. You take care of yourself and want for nothing. You can cook; you are what every man dreams of, so why wouldn't you think that I or any other man for that matter wouldn't want to settle down with you?"

"To be honest with you, I never really thought about being in a relationship since my college days. I guess I got so reserved with the thought of being with someone else at that time that I never even gave it anymore thought."

"Wow Vici, you've been out of college for what 8 to 10 years now and you mean to tell me that you reserved yourself for someone that you were hoping to notice you and so you put your life on hold?"

"You don't have to say it like that. I wanted to be with a certain person, and after a while I became so used to being single, that being in a relationship never really crossed my mind."

"I mean, men normally aren't as pressed to get into a relationship, but you're a lovely woman with everything going for you. I would assume that you would want a man to share that with."

Bryan gave Vici something to think about. She was all of these things and more and she did deserve to be happy. For years she had been putting herself on reserve for Ivyon, waiting in hopes that she would want to be in a committed relationship with her. Was this causing Vici to miss out on her life in hopes that Ivyon would want to make one with her?

"Bryan, I'm going on a two week vacation tomorrow, so when I come back we can discuss this further, if you'd like?"

"I would like that. Have a safe trip and don't skip out on our conversation."

"I won't, I promise. I'll see you in two weeks."

Vici had a lot to think about in the next two weeks. Here she finally had a man that was interested in her, not just her body, and she was about to blow him completely off. Now she had something and someone to consider.

DUBAI

All the women met up at the airport at 6:30 Sunday morning awaiting their arrival 25 hours later in Dubai. They each packed enough clothes to last them a month. All they talked about the entire plane ride down was actually being there and of course the crazy events that took place between Ivyon and Tina.

She hadn't spoken with Tessia about any of it yet, so she definitely had to catch her up on everything. She also had to inform Tessia about the break-up between her and Rufus, the build-up of Tina. Bringing Tessia current with the latest events of her life, she fast forwarded to the present; bringing her up to speed about Rufus and the fact that she loves him dearly and is actually considering giving him another chance.

Sitting in the background listening quietly, that was Vici's stamp of assurance that Ivyon was going back to Rufus, something that she wanted so desperately not to happen. She felt that maybe she should confess to Ivyon how she really felt about her. Maybe she would accept Vici's love over Rufus. She felt that she desperately had to do something if she stood any chance of being with Ivyon.

Once they arrived to the hotel, all the women went into their own rooms to unpack and settle down. Being on a flight for 25 hours will certainly make anyone tired. So they took naps and agreed to meet up within the next two hours in the main lobby for dinner and drinks.

Vici was dead tired like the rest of them; however, she couldn't sleep. She was heavily thinking of Ivyon and wanting to spend the rest of her life with her. Not just as a best friend but as her partner. She sat wondering what it would take to get Ivyon to agree to be with her and not Rufus. That would be a long shot, maybe she should consider being with Bryan and just let Ivyon move on with Rufus.

~~~~*~~~~

Tessia couldn't wait to get to her room and "unpack". Just the thought of finally being able to break away from the girls for a few hours was exactly what she needed. The sight of the beach they were staying on was absolutely breathtaking; she could never imagine this or even pay for it in a million years. Luckily she had Derek as Ivyon's dad, and he felt gracious enough to pay for their tickets. There was a reason behind Derek's gracious offer to send them on a vacation to an exotic country. Derek had been there a few days before to handle some business while he anticipated the arrival of Tessia. This was a vacation she desperately needed, not having some serious me time to herself in order to totally relax and just let go. Her husband really threw a wrench in her life, not thinking of his or her future. That was all in the past now, she had to learn how to move on and give herself a chance in the outside world. Dating seemed so far away from her reality, but it was something she really needed to do.

Once inside her room, she unpacked one suitcase that held all her yummy, exotic surprises. She had plans that no one on her trip knew about and hopefully no one would find out about. She took a quick shower and lotioned her body, adding a splash of perfume down the center of her body, behind her ears and between her thighs. Turning down the lights, she heard a knock on the door adjacent to her room;

heart ponding in her chest, not because this was her first time, but because she had been waiting for this for the past month. These get-togethers were rare and she had to make the best of them whenever they came about. This undoubtly would be the highlight of her trip, while everyone else was just excited to be in a foreign country. On the other side of the door was Derek standing in nothing but his birthday suite, dick standing at attention. Her Victoria's Secrets weren't even necessary at this point. Derek picked her up, kissing her deeply; he walked her over to the wall and inserted himself deeply inside her valley; heat coming from the both of their bodies as they shared in the same excitement and readiness to be with each other; trying to make each encounter better than or just as good as the last. Knowing they didn't have much time before Ivyon was going to come around, they got right down to business. Either of them performed as if they were in their late forties and early fifties, they performed like they were teenager's experiencing sex for the first time. No drugs were used to set the mood right, the fact that they wanted each other so bad sexually was the only drug they needed. They weren't in love and they knew their places with each other, they just gave each other what they desperately needed; ground breaking sex.

~~~~*~~~~

Ivyon opened the door to her room; let her bags fall to the floor as she fell to the bed, letting out a breath of exhaustion and appreciation to finally be in a bed. With so much on her mind, Ivyon just wanted to rest, nothing else. She didn't want to think of the crazy events that made up her life, she didn't want to think of the current space that she and Rufus shared, nor did she want to think of hurting Vici's feelings. She loved Vici with all her heart as a friend, but not how Vici wanted her to. She knew how Vici felt about her and how bad she wanted to be with her. Ivyon's heart belonged to Rufus, she knew it, Vici knew it and so did Rufus. It was just going to take some time for Ivyon to give herself completely back to him 100%. Until she did, she would get all of her sexual escapades out of her system so when that moment did come for her to devote herself to Rufus completely, it would be all about him. She tried that once before and he ended up sleeping with Tina, however, Ivyon knew there was nothing between them, still there was the hurt that Ivyon had to get over and that Rufus had to understand he caused her. Never wanting to feel that way again, Ivyon prepared herself for anything, protecting her heart from the worse of things that could happen.

At this point, everyone was feeling a little overwhelmed with whatever was going on in their private lives; they all just wanted to relax and have a good time. Let their lives at home stay at home. They were all going to have a good time no matter what. They were there for an entire two weeks; they had no choice but to have a great time. They had the beaches and the pools to visit, the night club's and the restaurants. They had a whole new exciting life waiting for them to embrace and accept.

BRONTE

After everyone took their time to themselves, they all met up in the main lobby as agreed to go out for dinner and drinks. They decided to just go out to the pool and have some girl talk over dinner and drinks. Nothing major, something small that they all needed after traveling for so long, no one really wanted to go out and be bothered after all. Being in the presence of each other was something good for them all at the moment. Bronte did feel a little lonely; she wanted to be in the presence of her lover. No one has ever made Bronte feel the way that she did when she was with Samone and she wanted to feel that way at all times. Bronte never thought in a million years that she would even ever be involved with another woman, until meeting Samone she knew with everything in her that she was straight, that she was interested in nothing but men. Samone surely changed her mind, made her start to question herself and her sexuality. There was nothing to feel bad about, she was grown and it was her life, she was enjoying it to the fullest. Whatever she stood to gain from it, she would.

"I wonder what Samone is doing at this very moment, if she's thinking about me as much as I am thinking of her. I know it's nothing but sex between us, she just makes me feel like I'm the only woman in the world when we're together and trust me there is no better feeling than that. I never had a guy put me on a pedestal or give me as much pleasure as she does, and I never want to lose that. Sex with her is memorable; it's more than sex with me. I feel the earth shake beneath my feet when I'm with her."

"Bronte? Did you hear a word I just said?"

"Huh? Ivyon, what are you talking about? I was in a daze; I didn't hear a damn thing."

"I see. Whatever his name is, he has definitely got you wide open."

"Girl, what are you talking about? Who has me wide open?"

"That's what I wanna know. Shit, give me some details. I would love to hear about somebody else's life besides the craziness that goes on in my own."

"Ivyon, I don't know what you are talking about. There is no guy that has me wide open."

"Hum, no guy? Tessia, cover your ears. Is it a woman that has you wide open?"
Ivyon and everyone else began to laugh, Ivyon just knew that Bronte wasn't exploring that side of nature, or so she thought.
"Being with a woman is a whole different ball game; it's in a league of their own. Big girls play that game; I don't think you're ready for that yet, Tay."

Vici joined in agreeing to what Ivyon said. "Bronte, it is truly a whole different experience. You have to know what you're getting into before you go down that road. In most cases traveling down that road, there's no turning back."

"Okay, first off ladies, I'm grown. I don't think I need a lesson in my sex life. If I want to date women, then I'll date women. If I want to date men, then I'll date men. If I want to date them both, then that's what I'll do."

"Oh well excuse us for trying to give you some knowledge. You're awfully testy about the subject, did I hit a nerve? Then again Bronte, you don't have to discuss your sex life with me if you don't want."

"Ivyon, don't take it that way, I didn't mean anything by it. I was just simply saying that I'm grown and I can take care of myself. If you must know, I am seeing someone that has me feeling some kind of way. It's nothing serious, we just please each other but it's a pleasure like no other. Should it matter if it's a man or woman? As long as I'm getting pleased and I'm not doing anything that can hurt me."

"No, actually it doesn't matter if it's a man or a woman, and you're right you are grown. I mean I am the little sister, but understand Bronte that I'm just trying to look out for you. Remember, I've been through more than a little bit, I know what types of things life can throw at you. I just wanna make sure that you're okay, that you don't get yourself into anything that you can't handle. So you keep jumping around it, so I take it that it is a woman that has you wide open? You don't have to say, however, just be careful; I know what it can bring you. If you ever need to talk or just need me for anything, I'm also here for you."

"Ivyon, I really appreciate that. If you must know, it is a woman. I've been seeing her for a couple months now and she just makes me feel like I've never felt before. I mean I love men and I would never give them up, but this woman has made me feel something that I never felt before. I mean she makes the world rumble underneath my feet. I've never felt this way before, and it took all of this time for me to feel this way and a woman was the one to make it happen."

At that moment Vici chimed in. "I totally understand where you're coming from. Men are wonderful creatures and trust me, they still make my toes curl, and it's just that women are more in tuned with women. We know our bodies and we know what we want. We know what makes us feel good and how to get things started. Don't get me wrong, you have your men out there that just automatically know what it takes to please a woman, that doesn't have a selfish bone in their bodies, but women know it best. I fell in love with a woman once that at first didn't know a thing about pleasing another woman, but we built up a friendship above all things. I love her to this day, and I really don't think that she knows it. I mean she has other things on her plate, and her attention is in a totally different direction. If given the chance, I would give anything I have to be with her, I mean anything. This is the type of stuff your sister is talking about, I'm sure of it. Women are more sensitive, emotional, understanding. They can disappoint you too, they can hurt you in every way a man can, they do everything a man can do in order to hurt you or to love you, it's just a whole different ball game when it comes down to it. Women know both sides of the game, so it's more complicated to get out of something with a female. Just be careful, protect your heart. If it's just a sex thing, then leave it at that, don't allow yourself to get caught up and always know when to walk away if it came down to it."

"Wow Vici, sounds like you're still in love with that woman. She took you through something."

"Because it's her, it's okay. I can honestly say that she is the love of my life without even knowing it. It didn't take much for me to fall for her. Her innocence was captivating, her body immaculate, she was soft and tender, yet strong all at the same time. She had me wide open and she didn't even know it. I introduced her into that world, taught her everything she knows and she enjoyed our sexual encounters very much, and that's all she wanted. I respected that about her and I never crossed that line, if making love to me when she needed was what she wanted, that was what I would give her. I had no choice, I loved her so much to be able to sacrifice what I really wanted from her, in order to give her what she wanted from me so I could keep her in my life. It was hard but believe me, it was well worth it."

Ivyon sipped her drink and looked away from the ladies. She knew Vici was talking about her, and she felt bad on the inside. She should not have invited her along for this trip because she knew the way she felt about her; however, she couldn't not bring her because ultimately she was her best friend. Ivyon got up from the table and sashayed away in the direction of the pool and took a dive into the deep end. Ivyon was feeling bad about the way Vici felt about her, she knew she could never give Vici what she wanted. Her heart belonged to Rufus, and even still, she couldn't risk losing Vici as a best friend to becoming her partner. She valued her friendship more and the love they had within it to let it go for anything that wasn't concrete. She took a couple of minutes to clear her head, swimming from one end of the pool to the next. When she came out to take a break, Vici's eyes were glued to Ivyon's face. Vici knew in that moment that Ivyon knew exactly who she was speaking about. Vici also knew that she made her feel uncomfortable, she knew she would never have Ivyon the way she wanted, but it was worth a try. Bronte was no fool, she followed the direction in which Vici eye's traveled, feeling a change in her vibe, she put two and two together.

"Vici, you mind if I ask you a question?"

"Sure, what's up?"

"You don't have to tell me if you don't want, you can tell me it's none of my damn business. Are you in love with my sister, is Ivyon the one you would give anything to be with?"

Vici looked Bronte in her eyes, took a sip of her drink and walked off. Never answering the question, she didn't even entertain it. Under her breathe Bronte whispered "I guess that answered my question. WOW."

All the ladies went about their own ways, leaving Bronte there with much to think about. The girls were right, however, she wanted Samone in more ways than a little bit. She wanted to be with her every minute of every hour of the day. She didn't care if Samone didn't feel the same way; she would make her love her eventually. Bronte had never felt this way about anyone in her life before and she loved the way it felt, this woman made her feel alive again. Bronte decided she would give Samone a call to hear the sweet sounds that made up her voice.

"Hey Samone, how are you?"

"I'm fine Bronte. How are you? Is everything alright? It's the middle of the night."

"Shit Samone, I'm sorry. I didn't realize the time difference. I didn't want anything, I'll call you later."

"It's okay, I'm awake now. What's up sweetie? Are you having withdrawals from my loving?"

"Actually, I am. I wish you were here with me now. It's so exotic and romantic here. This would be the perfect place for us to explore each other. Everywhere you turn puts you in the mood for love making."

"Wow, sounds dreamy. Now that you mentioned it, I wish I was there too. I can imagine being in one of those warm pools with your legs wrapped around my waist and my fingers deep inside you causing your own personal set of waves. Hearing your moans turns me on even more causing me to explode."

Bronte was now happy that she made the call. Even though Samone wasn't there with her, she could get a visual of her doing all kinds of things to her. Bronte still sitting at the patio table, not having a care in the world, she let her fingers travel beneath the panty line of her bathing suit to slip inside her moistness. Bronte could feel the intensity; she wanted Samone right there with her to take her to where she needed to be. She wanted to feel the touch of Samone up against her body, she wanted Samone's fingers inside of her instead of her own, and she wanted to feel her breath on the nape of her neck, her tongue in her valley. She didn't have any of that at the moment, so she would have to settle for phone sex thousands of miles away. She thought of her touching her everywhere, in places she couldn't reach outside at the patio table. Her body was hot for the touch of Samone; she could actually feel the heat coming off her. Samone knew how she made Bronte feel, and she did it with such ease and intensity because she always imagined it was Ivyon. Samone pleased Bronte as much as she possibly could using the thought of Ivyon. Was it wrong? Probably so, but she didn't care one way or the other.

TINA

Tina enjoyed pleasing Bronte and making her cum, but it was nothing like the real thing. Ivyon turned her completely out, she never was this way, she was never even interested in women until she met Ivyon. She could see how Bronte could be so turned out and hooked on the drug she was offering her, because her sister offered it to her years ago. That was without a doubt the best love making experience in her life all at the hands of a woman. She paid careful attention to the things that Ivyon used to do to her and teach her. Now she was doing all these things and more to Bronte. She learned a few new tricks that she would love to teach Ivyon. If only she could think of a way to get Ivyon to love her and leave that damn Rufus. Tina tried one time before to get Rufus out of the picture but it just didn't work. Yeah he was gone for a while, now he was back in the picture. Tina couldn't understand what Rufus had on Ivyon that would make her take him back after she caught him fucking her on the desk of his office. Sure they are truly back together but it's just a matter of time before they are a couple again.

Being in Dubai bought Tina closure to Ivyon, she just had to play it close, not wanting Ivyon or Bronte to spot her. She couldn't have Ivyon that far away from her for that long amount of time. Even if she couldn't touch or taste her, she still needed to be able to see her. She periodically made her way around Ivyon, she watched her at the airport, she watched her as they arrived to the hotel, she watched her as she slept before meeting the girls for dinner, and she made sure she watched her when she took her swim. She wanted so bad to be the pool that Ivyon was diving into, she wished she could lick her dry. No one knew she was there and she planned to keep it that way. Being in love was hard, especially when the one you love doesn't love you back. So naturally Tina knew she had to do whatever it took to make Ivyon love her as much as she loved Ivyon.

Being in Dubai with Ivyon and Bronte was a tease, knowing that she couldn't be with either of them at that time. Usually she would just be satisfied with pleasing Bronte and thinking she was Ivyon, but she was hurting herself more and more by being that close to both of them and not being able to have either of them. Tina was thought of to be on the crazy side, she stalked Ivyon and she didn't think there was anything wrong with it. She met this girl years ago and she has become addicted to her ever since. No matter what she does to try to get over Ivyon, to get her out of her system, she can't. It's almost as if Ivyon was a drug and Tina was still searching for that first high, Ivyon was her own personal brand of heroin and she never wanted to be clean. She was no doubt a drug addict for this woman, and just like any other drug addict addicted to drugs, she would do whatever she had to do to get her next high. No other drug would do it for her, not cocaine, not marijuana, not ecstasy pills, not Bronte, nothing but Ivyon could give her that high that she so desperately needed.

She had an itch that needed scratching, just like a dope fiend, she had that itch, that twitch, that burn, that yearning sensation that only Ivyon could take away. She's been in withdrawal for so long that she could barely keep it together. She had a taste of her the night she broke in and pretended to be Vici, but that wasn't good enough. She needed Ivyon to need her back, she wanted Ivyon to scream her name; she wanted Ivyon to tell her that she loved her and no one else. If she approached Ivyon here, she ran the risk of being arrested in a foreign country at least if she were back at home, she knew she would have a better chance of getting out and that she would be on U.S. soil. At the rate Tina was going, nothing was impossible to her when it came to Ivyon. She would go to any height, any extent to get the woman she loved to love her back, she just didn't know how to properly go about doing it. She found her stuck between the woman she made love to and the woman she loved and wanted to make love to. It's nothing like the real thing, Ivyon had everything she needed, wanted, and desired, but how would she get Ivyon to realize that she was the one for her; that they belonged together, to share in a life of pure happiness and bliss. In Tina's mind, no one could love Ivyon the way Tina could and she was determined to show her.

Tina realized just how bad she actually had it for Ivyon, but there was nothing she could do except be with her. No one could fill that void that Ivyon left in her heart. "I was never like this before Ivyon came into my life. I was quiet and didn't bother anyone; I had a life of my own where everything was simple and straight forward. Now, none of this makes sense to me, I'm chasing a woman that I may likely never have, but the other part of me won't allow me to move on. It's crazy; it's as if I'm battling with someone else in my head, as if someone else is calling the shots. "I AM CALLING THE SHOTS AND YOU KNOW IT. SO STOP YOUR WHINING AND JUST DO WHAT I TELL YOU." Tina swung around to see who was talking to her, since she was in her room all alone, or so she thought.

"Who said that? Who are you? Why won't you leave me alone?"

"YOU KNOW WHO I AM. I AM YOU, AND YOU KNOW YOU WANT THE SAME THINGS I WANT, YOU ARE JUST TOO DAMN SCARED TO GO AFTER

THEM. THAT'S WHY YOU CREATED ME,
MICHELLE. SO I COULD DO EVERYTHING FOR
YOU."

Tina put her hands up over her ears to try to block out the
voice. "I don't know you, what are you talking about. I
don't want this."

"SURE YOU DO. LIKE I SAID YOU'RE JUST TOO
AFRAID TO GO AFTER IT."

"What are you talking about? I never asked for any of this.
I was a good girl, I minded my own business, I stayed to
myself, and I enjoyed my life."

"THAT'S EXACTLY WHY YOU WENT OUT TO THE
CLUB THAT NIGHT SEEKING SOME EXCITEMENT
RIGHT? BECAUSE YOU'RE A GOOD GIRL? SURE
YOU ARE A GOOD GIRL WHO WANTS CERTAIN
THINGS THAT SHE IS TOO AFRAID OF GOING
AFTER HERSELF. YOU NEEDED ME TO GO AFTER
ALL THESE THINGS FOR YOU, THAT'S WHY YOU
CREATED ME. REMEMBER, YOU CAME TO ME
CYRING, SEEKING HELP; TO HELP YOU GET ALL
THE THINGS YOU WANTED. I DIDN'T COME TO
YOU, I WAS FINE, BURIED DEEP IN YOUR
SUBCONSCIENCE, YOU SOUGHT ME OUT."

"No, I don't believe you, I never sought anyone out. All
these things that you make me do aren't me. I would never
do these types of things if you weren't in my head
controlling me. This is all you; these are all the things you
want to do."

"SO YOU DO KNOW WHO I AM?"

"No, I don't. However, I know you're not real; it's all in my head. All I have to do is continue to tell myself that you're not real and you'll get from out of my head."

"YOU CAN TRY BUT I'M NOT GOING ANYWHERE. I CAN'T GO ANYWHERE BECAUSE I AM YOU!"

"I regret that night I went to the club, maybe if I'd stayed home, you wouldn't be in my head right now."

"YOU COULDN'T HELP YOURSELF. YOU WANTED TO BE IN THAT CLUB THAT NIGHT, YOU SAT THERE ALL ALONE LOOKING OUT OF PLACE, HOPING THAT SOMEONE WOULD APPROACH YOU. GUESS WHAT? IT HAPPENED. YOU WATCHED IVYON GETTING FUCKED AGAINST THAT WALL AS IF IT WAS YOU. "

"No, I didn't ask for any of that. I regret it all. I regret watching her, I regret her catching my eye, and I regret her coming over to my table. I regret the kiss, the licking, the fingering, the strap-on, the bending me over the table. I regret how hard she made me cum. I regret it all. I never asked for any of it, it was you. You wanted to be with her, you sought her out. You thought she was sexy and wanted to be with her. It was all you, none of me, you just took over my mind and my body and made me do things that I would never do. Now look at me, I'm stuck. I can't get this woman out of my head, I can't move forward, I can't breathe without thinking about this woman and it's all because of you."

"NO IT'S ALL BECAUSE OF YOU. YOU DON'T GET IT DO YOU? I AM YOU; I ONLY DO WHAT YOU TELL ME TO DO. I DON'T ACT ON MY OWN, HOW

COULD I? YOU HAVE CONTROL OVER THE BODY AND WHO YOU WANT TO BE WITH; I JUST MAKE IT HAPPEN FOR YOU BECAUSE YOU'RE TOO AFRAID. YOU NEVER WANTED ANY OF THIS? REALLY? THAN WHY DID YOU MAKE ME UP? I'M ONLY HERE BECAUSE OF YOU, WHERE ELSE WOULD I COME FROM?"

Tina looked at herself in the mirror, shook her head and sat in a corner to cry. She couldn't believe what she was going through, she needed help and she knew it. She just couldn't bring herself to get any. Even though she knew what she was putting herself through, she was still in love with Ivyon and wanted desperately to be with her. She opened that gate a long time ago, and now she had to walk through it.

IVYON

After a few hard days in Dubai, Ivyon decided to let everything go and just try to live. She was tired of everything bad happening to her, causing her to be depressed. It was time for her to LET GO and LET GOD. She thought long and hard about her life, her past, her present, and her future. She learned that she had to be grounded in her past, to survive her present to make for a promising future. No longer was she going to allow people to hurt her, to steal her joy or to bring her down. Her spirit was controlled by a higher being and shined from a brighter light. She finally made room in her heart to forgive Rufus and to be his woman, she was tired of her sexcapes, and she just wanted to be with him. He completed her life and she knew it, she was just being stubborn because he had hurt her so badly. She changed her life for him and he went and slept with someone else that was like the ultimate betrayal. But she had to swallow her pride; it was time to move on. Ivyon would make this deal with her dad here in Dubai to open their new restaurant and from there; she was going home to her man. It was truly time for her to be happy.

"Hey dad, what are you up to today?"

"Hey precious, not too much. I was thinking about going down to the pool side, to relax, maybe take a swim and have some lunch. Just enjoy the sights, you know?"

"Sounds good. Relaxation is always a good thing. Being able to clear your mind or think things through."

"Well why don't you come and join me then? I'll be down on the pool side in about an hour. Is that good for you?"

"Ok, that's fine. That gives me enough time to fully wake up and get myself together. I'll meet you there."

With that Ivyon got out of bed, showered, got dressed and pulled her back into a pony. She was making her way out of the door when her cell phone rang. It was a number she wasn't familiar with so she sent it to voicemail. Two steps closer to the door, her phone rang again from the same number. This time she answered.

"Hello"
Nothing, all she heard was breathing.
"Hello"
Again, nothing.
"Who is this?"
Breathing.
"Look, find someone else's phone to play on; I don't have time for this."

"Don't you fucking hang up on me BITCH, all you've put me through?"

"Who the hell is this?"

"Oh you don't know? Can't you tell my voice? Or was I that much of a non-factor to you that you don't remember? I bet you remember me sucking on that pussy, making you scream out "VICI."

Ivyon felt her heart drop into the pit of her stomach.

"Tina?"

"Oh, now you remember?"

"Tina what the hell do you want? How did you even get this number?"

"Ivy, my sweet, sweet Ivy. I know everything about you. I even know what you're wearing right now. You look so cute and girly with your ponytail. I love it, well you make anything look good, and I do mean anything."

"What the hell do you mean? Are you watching me? Fuck that, are you here? How the fuck did you know where I would be? Something is seriously wrong with you, you really should seek some help you crazy BITCH."

"Oh, I'm the crazy one? You like to go around fucking women and men that you don't know whenever you please, and then get amnesia when they approach you for more. You let anyone stick anything in you just so you can come, but I'm the crazy one? Who do you think really needs to seek help? You're addicted to sex, but I need help?"

"You know what Tina; I never regret anything in my life, because if I do, I'll miss the lesson that's in it. You were a side piece of mine that could handle being a side piece. The golden rule in being a side piece is to know your role and your place. I have no use for you anymore, so bitch stay in your place. I licked your pussy so good that you became an addict, I got news for you. People become addicted to lots of things, and if they really want help, they have places and institutions called rehab, bitch go get it. Did you honestly think I would make a life with you? I mean really, you let me "a total stranger" spread you eagle style across a bar table and fuck you with a dildo. So which of us really needs the help? If you're going to play the game, learn how to play it right. You could have walked away at any time, but no you wanted this warm, thick tongue in that pussy so bad that you would come wherever I called you. So which of us is addicted? I'm through with you, you are in my past and I'm leaving all things that have no meaning or existence there, so have a good life, and really look into getting some help."

With that Ivyon hung up that phone and smiled to herself. She was finally taking control over the things she used to let affect her life. Ivyon looked at her phone and tossed it on her bed and walked out the door.

~~~*~~~

"Hey dad. Wow, you ordered without me?"

"No, honey I took the liberty and ordered you food and a glass of wine also, mine just happened to come out first."

"Hmmm, what do you have? It smells really good." Ivyon reached around a grabbed his fork to have a taste. "It tastes really good, too."

"It's smoked salmon."

Ivyon and Derek spent the afternoon together talking and going over their plans for their restaurant. They had great plans and ideas together once they actually had the chance to sit down and brainstorm. They had all the logistics together, all the cash flow, the building, and the floor plan. They had everything planned out down to the master chef. By the time they were through going over everything, meeting the third party who they were going to partner with, it was time for dinner. Their business was done here and as far as Ivyon was concerned, so was her vacation. She was ready to go home and get her man.

BRONTE

Everybody seemed to be having a good time until they weren't any more. I'm here on a secluded island with no one to talk to because everybody is in their own feelings, I'm horny and I'm stuck in a world wind inside my head. I want to be back at home with Samone, just to feel her hands and kisses all over my body right now; I need some love. Not just any kind of love,
Samone is the only one that can do me right. She knows every inch, every curve, and every crack of my body. I don't have to tell her what to do to me because she already knows. Let me get out of this room before I drive myself crazy.

Bronte walked down to the bar area to get a drink and clear her mind. She ordered a strawberry margarita and just relaxed, until somebody walked past her handing flyers for a party that tonight. Bronte needed some excitement badly, she was missing everything and the result of that was boredom. Bronte overlooked the flyer and realized it was an advertisement of a swinger's party later on that night. Having nothing else better to do, Bronte decided she would go just to check it out.

Getting ready for the party, all she kept hearing in her head was the voice of Ivyon and Vici telling her that it could be a dangerous game to play if you really didn't know what you were getting yourself into. Keeping that in mind, she knew she had to be extremely careful at this party. She wouldn't know anyone there and she didn't even want to tell Ivyon that she was
going, because she was afraid of Ivyon's reaction. "Look at me, I'm the big sister and I'm scared of her." Bronte knew all too well why she was afraid of Ivyon, but she just could

not allow Ivyon to look at her in that way, even though Ivyon was bisexual, it didn't matter. Bronte was certainly unsure of her sexuality, even though she indulged in both sexes, and she knew which one turned her on more. She didn't want to be looked at in that manner; she wasn't comfortable enough in her own skin to come to terms with it just yet. As she put her clothes on and walked toward the door, she debated within herself to leave Ivyon a note to at least tell her where she'd be just in case anything happened to her, but she decided against it.

Fifteen minutes later after struggling to find her way through the
city with no lock, she decided to catch a cab. Catching a cab was the easy part, getting to this party that she now found out was in a secluded part of town that was sort of forbidden, the cab driver warned her of where she was going, but she didn't care. Once they pulled up, all she saw were bright flashing lights and all she heard was sweet seductive music blaring from the speakers. She paid the driver and requested for him to return within the hour for her. The driver pleaded with her not to go inside, "This is very bad here in our country, these parties are against the law. They get raided all the time, please Ms. American lady do not go inside. Bad things happen inside." Bronte looked away from him to the door; she put her head down as she debated with herself about going inside. She contemplated and contemplated before she finally decided to go inside and see what all the fuss was about.

"Please come back for me within an hour." With that Bronte got out of the car and went inside. Once inside she was pleasantly surprised by what she saw. There were beds everywhere surrounded by sheer curtains, servers walking around with drinks, serving them to any and everyone who wanted a drink. There were tables lined with exotic colored cloths, filled with assorted colored, multi-sized condoms everywhere. One thing she could tell there was that they did practice safe sex. The atmosphere gave her a soothing, relaxed feeling, made her feel like everything was going to be alright. She didn't feel dirty or like she didn't belong, she actually felt welcomed.

She made her rounds, walking through the entire building just to get a better feel for everything while she was there. Everyone was well mannered, nobody came up to her and just grabbed on her or disrespected her, a few people approached her with nice conversation but she just wasn't interested in them. She'd find someone eventually that she would want to engage with. Time past by as she sat in the background and had a few drinks. She looked down at her watch and realized her cab would
be back in 30 minutes and she hadn't had any real excitement. These women were breathtaking, something about their smooth, brown skin made her want every last one of them. Deep in thought she never even noticed a women come and sit beside her, until she felt her hand caress her skin.

Whipping her head around, Bronte said in a surprise, "uh excuse me."

"Oh, I'm sorry I scared you, I tried talking to you but you were deep in thought, so I wanted to get your attention."

"Oh, I'm sorry, that was very rude of me. I hadn't realized anyone was over here, you're right I was deep in thought. Please forgive me." Bronte extended her hand, "I'm Bronte."

"Oh it's no problem. Pleased to meet you, I'm Shakira."

Shakira could tell that Bronte was a little nervous, that this had to
have been her first time. So before she scared her too much, she
talked to Bronte for what seemed like hours. Bronte had forgotten all about her cab waiting for her. Shakira made her feel extremely comfortable, comfortable enough to walk her over to their own private bed.

"Bronte I think you are so beautiful and sexy and I would be honored to taste you." Bronte was starting to get a little nervous. The only woman she'd ever been with was Samone; she wouldn't know what to do. Shakira could see the nervousness in her face.

"Don't worry, I won't hurt you, nor will I do anything that you don't
want me to do. My husband usually joins me at these types of parties, but I don't think you're ready for that."

"Oh my, you're married?"

"Yes, I am but don't worry, he doesn't have to participate. I actually want you all to myself anyway."

Bronte was so excited about this woman, she felt her panties soiled. Her clitoris was jumping the entire time as she thought about all the things this brown beauty could do to her. The more she listened to her seductive voice, the more she wanted to feel this woman's hands all over her.

"I am very nervous and I don't want to be selfish by just letting you please me."

"Oh, don't worry, I don't find you to be selfish at all."

Shakira slipped her hand under Bronte's dress, running her fingers up and down Bronte's thighs, watching Bronte's expression she knew she was doing something that Bronte liked. So she went a little further, she outlined the crouch of Bronte's panties and felt just how wet they were. This boosted her ego, confirming that she was doing just what Bronte wanted her to do. With her index finger, Shakira slid Bronte's panties to the side as she traced her from her inner lips to her clitoris playing in her wetness. She pulled her finger out and it was submerged in her juices. She licked her finger just to see just how sweet Bronte really was, Bronte turned out to be to her satisfaction and more, so she stuck her entire finger into her mouth and sucked all of her essence off it. Shakira enjoyed her taste so much she wanted more.

"Go ahead and lie back for me."

Bronte did what she asked nervously taking her time to lie back.

Shakira reached up her dress and pulled her panties down. She slid her hand down Bronte's silky legs and propped them up on the bed; she faded away from Bronte's eyesight. Bronte no longer saw her but within a matter of seconds she felt her warm tongue on her clit as her warm, smooth lips surrounded it. Bronte bucked out of pure satisfaction just that quickly. Accepting her reaction, Shakira sucked really tight on to Bronte's clit and quickly darted her tongue in and out of the opening of Bronte's tunnel. Bronte was in so much orgasmic bliss, she couldn't help but to grab and pull at Shakira's hair.

As Shakira indulged deeper and deeper with her tongue and now fingers, Bronte lost total control, she screamed to the top of lungs as she experienced an uncontrollable shake.

She had never received so much pleasure in her life, not even from Samone. Had she known she had to fly to another continent to receive this much pleasure, she would have planned a trip years ago. Shakira ate Bronte this way for all of about 10 minutes before she came up and kissed her, allowing Bronte to taste her own nectar. In the mist of it all, Shakira's husband found her and walked over hoping he could join in. He walked over and leaned in for a kiss from Bronte and Shakira stopped him.

"No Hareem, I want her all to myself. This is her first time; I don't think she can handle us both."

Bronte opened her eyes, and what she saw standing above her was a God. Nice tall, olive-skinned, dark haired, muscular man that smelled soooooo good. Hareem looked down at Bronte and saw something in her eyes, he leaned in and kissed her nice and slow. When he came up Bronte's eyes were still closed as she let out a deep, refreshing breath. Hareem asked her, "Can I have a taste?" Bronte could do nothing but shake her head yes.

Shakira smiled as she raised Bronte's dress above her head and fully removed all her clothes. Shakira straddled Bronte and cupped her breast in both hands as she suckled her nipples one at a time with Hareem between Bronte's legs tasting her sweet flavor. Bronte thought she would lose her mind as she was in a world wind of ecstasy. Hareem was so excited by her taste, his penis became instantly erect, he felt that if she could taste this good, she must feel wonderful. With her permission, Hareem inserted himself into her warm, sweet, wet secret tunnel. Bronte was so tight and velvety that Hareem came instantly; something that has never happened to him before, not even with his wife. Hareem had to regain his composure, he walked over to his wife and she immediate inserted his penis into her mouth and began to swivel around his shaft faster and faster while cupping his sack, massaging them gently in her hands until he stood at attention again.

This time Shakira wanted to fill him inside her, she didn't want to be the only one not receiving any pleasure. She got in between Bronte's legs again lapping up all of her sweetness while her husband inserted himself in her from behind. Both ladies were moaning in pure pleasure. Bronte got up enough courage to finally want to participate. All of them got up to change positions; Bronte straddled Hareem from behind while Shakira lay flat on her back allowing Bronte easy access to taste her. Bronte couldn't believe how good this woman taste in her mouth; she'd never tasted anything like it before.

They shared in each other's bliss to the wee hours of the night. Everyone tasted everyone and enjoying orgasm after orgasm. Of course by the time they were done, Bronte's cab was no longer outside waiting for her. She found herself standing alone outside scared to death. Not knowing how she would get back to the hotel, not evening knowing where it was. Bronte crossed her arms over her chest and started to walk in no direction in particular. Bronte saw headlights coming up behind her; she was getting scared, when finally she heard a horn and someone called out her name.

"Bronte."

She turned around in fear and noticed it was Shakira and Hareem calling out to her. She was relieved, she no longer had the fear that someone would drag her off onto one of these deserted roads, rape and kill her.

"Bronte, are you okay sweetie, do you need a ride

somewhere?"

"Oh my God, yes. I asked my cab to come back an hour after he dropped me off. But I guess time had gotten away from me, so naturally he wasn't here to pick me back up. I can't blame him. I'm staying at the Burj Al Arab Jumeriah Hotel."

"Really? You chose an awesome hotel to stay in." They drove in silence for the remainder of the ride. Once they reached her hotel, Shakira said "Bronte, my husband and I really enjoyed your company tonight. If you're ever in town again and want to get together, here's my card. Just give me a call. As a matter of fact, you give me a call in advance and we'll make arrangements to have you stay with us."

Bronte put her head down, smiled and said "Thanks Shakira and Hareem, I'll keep that in mind. And thank you for bringing me back to my hotel. I don't know what I would have done without you."

With that Bronte walked to her room, showered and went to sleep.

VICI

Back at home from a 2 week vacation of heaven. After unpacking and settling in, Vici poured herself a cold, tall glass of Merlot. She went out onto her back patio and lay across her deep wine colored chaise lounge chair, overlooking her swimming pool 10 feet below. Thoughts were racing through her head about her life and Ivyon's life.

She so desperately wanted to be with Ivyon, but Ivyon wanted to be with Rufus. Vici really understood that now after vacationing with her in Dubai. Vici now had to allow herself to be what she started out being and what she intended to be to Ivyon, which was her best friend. She had to step back and let her live her life without any distractions from Vici. Her friend deserves to be happy, to have someone love her whole heartedly. Ivyon grew up around people hurting and disappointing her, Vici didn't want to be one of those people. She realized that Ivyon had suffered enough in her life, and she needed so much more. As much as it would hurt, Vici realized she hurt Ivyon also by not being the true friend she needed her to be and wanting Ivyon all to herself. She had to step back and let Ivyon go, deep in thought she heard her doorbell ring.

"Ugh, I forgot that Bryan was coming over, I really don't want any company today." Vici got up from her comfort zone on her chaise and went to answer the door. Opening the door, Bryan was standing there with his hands full of bags.

"Wow, what's all this?"

"Well I know you just had a long 2 weeks of fun and an even longer plane ride home, so I thought I would come and pamper you. I've brought a different variety of groceries with me because I wasn't sure on what you might want. Oh, and by the way, these are for you."

Bryan handed her two dozen multi-colored, long steamed roses and walked past her toward her kitchen after planting a soft kiss on her cheek. Vici looked shocked as she looked at the roses and followed him into the kitchen.

"Bryan, thank you, these are beautiful."

"Beautiful roses for my beautiful rose."

"So what do you have in the bags? Looks like a lot. Do I need to eat all that food?"

"Well like I said, I didn't know what you may have been in the mood for, so I came prepared. So here are you choice's, I have steak, lamb, chicken, and just in case you had a taste for seafood, I brought salmon also. Now the veggies, you don't get to choose from, but I promise you will not be disappointed. I've also brought a selection of red and white wines and I can see that you have already started on a white, so we'll go with that."

"Wow, I don't know what to say, there is so much to choose from."

"Well how about you don't say anything? You go back out onto the balcony and I'll come and get you when I finish. How about that?"

"Ok, that's fine."

Vici went back out onto the balcony and curled up onto her chair, soaked in the sun and closed her eyes. Going back to her thoughts about her life and the life of her best friend, she started to reminisce about the times they spent together throughout their life. She posed the question to herself "what's more important, having her in my bed, or having her in my life forever as my best friend?" In that instant she knew what she had to do, quietly smiling to herself while allowing the sun to kiss her face, Vici drifted off to sleep.

An hour later Vici awoke to sweet aromas of different scents. She had waken up from what seemed like hours of sleep, until she looked down at her watch and realized she had only slept for an hour. Grabbing her glass of wine off the table beside her, she realized it was no longer chilled, but hot, she needed a refill. She grabbed her glass and walked into the house, the scenery that was displayed captured her breath and her heart. This view was magnificently breathtaking, her entire downstairs was illuminated by candlelight, and she went from room to room to experience a new level of comfort and warmth. She came up into the dining room where she caught Bryan lighting the last of the candles on top of the table.

"Bryan, this is just, oh my God....I'm speechless, lost for words."

"That was the reaction I was looking for, "the wow factor". So I take it that I've succeed?"

"Oh my God."

A bright smile across his face, Bryan shook his head assured and said "yeah, I succeeded."

"Well Ms. Vici, shall we eat?" Bryan took her by the hand and led her to the table where his spread was diligently laid out. Hand covering her mouth, Vici was in total shock as Bryan pulled her chair out and instructed her to take a seat. Vici followed his orders and dropped her hand, looked up at Bryan and said "this is truly amazing".

"Thank you. I didn't know what you wanted to eat so I took the liberty and cooked it all. You can choose from lamb chops drizzled with a honey and lemon sauce topped with basil, grilled steak and mushrooms in a red wine sauce, roasted garlic grilled chicken breast, or seared salmon fillets. Now you have no choice with your vegetables, I carefully chose these. You have a selection of sautéed asparagus with sun dried tomatoes, sweet string beans and/or fried cabbage, or grilled squash and grilled zucchini. So what would like to have?"

"Damn Bryan, what are you trying to do to me? This is just too much; I don't know what to choose. I don't even know if I can choose just one."

"How about this, I give you just a taste of all your meats with a small portion of your vegetables?"

"Okay, that sounds good."

Bryan prepared her plate with a small portion of it all; he replenished her glass of wine with a more chilled Merlot, poured over frozen pineapples and cantaloupe. After setting her plate in front of her, he held her hands and bowed his head to bless their food. "Oh heavenly Father who art thou in heaven, we come to you in a moment of prayer and appreciation. God we want to thank you for all the blessings you have bestowed upon us and we hope that you will continue to bless us in our time of need. God we thank you for providing us with this wonderful food and we ask that you bless it to nourish our bodies and lighten our spirits, in your son Jesus Christ's name we pray. AMEN."

"Bryan, that was wonderful. Just when I think it can't possibly get any better, you surprise me again."

"That is my goal, to keep you surprised and satisfied. Now go ahead and tell me how you like your food."

"Well aren't you going to join me?"

"No baby, I'll eat after you've eaten and I know that you are satisfied."

Vici just looked at him, smiled and shook her head before she took the first bite. All she could think was "Ivyon is the only person that would cook for me like this. Maybe God sent this man to be for my own piece of Heaven so Ivyon and I both can finally be happy. If this man continues to cook for me like this, I won't need Ivyon's cooking, good God almighty this food is scrumptious." Vici finished her meal and Bryan walked her upstairs to a candlelit bubble bath, where he disrobed her and held her hand as she carefully climbed up the steps and stepped inside her tub.

"Now you relax here while I get a bite to eat and clean the downstairs."

Vici laid her back against her bath pillow and closed her eyes. She soaked up the evening that she never wanted to end. She was so deep in thought, she never even heard Bryan come back into the bathroom handing her a fresh glass of wine. She watched him as he stripped down completely naked and got in the tub behind her. He massaged her shoulders for a bit and told her to lie back on his chest and relax. They stayed this way in silence until the water became cold. They got out of the tub and got into the separate stand up shower where Bryan carefully washed her body from head to toe, taking extra care with her personal parts. After he was finished, Vici returned the favor. They dried off and Bryan wrapped her body in an extra-large, plush bath towel and carried her to her bed.

Bryan laid her across her bed on her stomach and slowly poured warmed massage oils down the spine of her back, carefully catching it in between her fingers and deeply rubbing it into her skin. He gave her a deep tissue, pressure massage from the nap of her neck to the sole of her feet. After he was done, he carefully turned her over and gave her front side the same treatment. Knowing that she was now satisfied and relaxed, Bryan lay behind her in the spoon position, wrapped his arms around her body, kissed her behind her ear and whispered the sweet words "good night my love." As extremely turned on as she was, Vici couldn't ask for a more perfect night. She lay there in the arms of the man she now realized she loved, and she fell asleep.

~~~*~~~

"I didn't really feel like dealing with Bryan yesterday, but God knows, if that man can make me feel that good all the time, I would never want to leave his side. I never knew what true love felt like, and if that's what it feels like, then I would want to keep it forever. I know that I told him that would talk when I came back, I would tell him whatever he wanted to know, but when he showed up yesterday, he didn't put any pressure on me; he didn't even bring it up. He came here to cater to me, to make me feel loved. Ivyon, this man made me feel like a queen, like I was the only woman in the world. He never once asked about my trip, about my past, or about anything actually. He came here and lit my entire house with candles, and he cooked for me, we bathed together and he gave me the best massage I've ever had, and then he cuddled with me until I fell asleep in his arms. He never even tried to have sex with me, and I would have given it to him like a porn star the way he treated me last night."

"That is what you call intimacy. Vici, I really think this man loves you. You should give him a chance, I mean I know that starting something new can be scary, especially when you are putting your heart into it, but how would you ever know how it will be if you don't try it? I know that this will be the first heterosexual, serious relationship you've had in years but maybe God waited for a reason to send this man to you now. Look at me, just when I thought things would never get right for me, he sent me Rufus. I know that he cheated on me with that crazy bitch Tina, but I know he really didn't mean that. I believe in my heart that Rufus truly didn't intend to hurt me, Tina was out to get me for her own selfish reasons and I think that she set Rufus up to get back at me. Even though it was his decision to part take or not, and he did, but I don't think that it was intentional. I love Rufus and I want to make this work with him, because like you, I've never known what true love was until I met that man, and I'll be damned if I let it go."

"So do I hear wedding bells Ivyon?"

"Laughing, Ivyon said "if he popped the question, I would definitely say yes. What about you? I mean I know it's still fresh and all, but if this man can make you feel that way then it sounds like he's a keeper."

"To be honest Ivy, I don't think I got that far with him yet. I mean he still doesn't know about my past, and I'm not sure that when I tell him, he'll still feel the same way as he does right now. Who's to say if he won't find me disgusting or just can't handle being with a woman with my sexual experience and past, what would I do then?"

"Well my suggestion is to tell him, and let him decide if after knowing he still wants to be with you. You're not a bad person Vici, you're a woman that takes control in her own life and lives how she wants. You do what you want, but you do it safely, you're not hurting anyone or yourself, you take of yourself and you don't ask anyone for anything. You're a very successful woman, you have your own business, you own your own home and cars, and you take care of yourself. We just love sex, and have fun. Who's to say there's anything wrong with that? However, if we truly love these men and they are who we want to be with, then we have to maintain control."

"Ivy, it's not hard for me to be faithful, that's not the problem. I don't want to get all hooked up into him and he rejects me."

"Vici, I really don't think that he will. I can't say for sure, but why would he put himself through all that if he weren't going to stick it out with you."

"Well I guess we'll see tonight. We have a date, I don't know where we're going or what he actually has in mind, but you better answer your phone when I call or text me back if I text you."

"Girl, you know I will. No matter what I'm doing I always make time for my BFF. Now stop being scared and go ahead and get ready."

~~~*~~~

Ivyon and Vici exchanged hugs before Ivyon kissed her cheek and wished her luck. "It'll be ok, honey, trust me." After Ivyon left, Vici pressed her hair out and got dressed. She was nervous, but what could she do? Run away from her problems? No she couldn't, she would just have to face the music and deal with it. Vici put on a sleeveless black dress that cut low in the cleavage area, black Red Bottom 8 inch heels, pearl neckless and bracelet. Bryan got to her house and she walked to the car, he opened up her door for her and kissed her gently before she got in and told her how beautiful she looked. He took her to a nice 5 star restaurant that was quiet and quaint. Bryan felt blessed to be in her presence, he hadn't felt this way about a woman in a very long time and he only could hope that Vici felt the same way about him.

"Bryan, this is a nice restaurant. Where did you hear about this?"

"A friend of mine told me about it. He said they have some of the best customer service and they make a killer Sangria, so I figured we'd try it out."

Vici could no longer take it; she was driving herself crazy over the thought that if he would still want her after she told him her life story. So she figured since he wouldn't ask, she would just tell.

"Bryan, I know I told you that we would talk when I got back, and I would tell you whatever you wanted to know. So what is it that you want to know?"

"Vici, there is nothing that I want to know about your past. Your past is just that, "your past", now I hope that you will give me the chance to create a present with you that will lead to a future."

Vici again was speechless, lost for words. She didn't know how to react or what to say. She looked at Bryan with confusion and worry in her eyes.

"Vici, I know that all of this may be new to you, but I promise I am not here to cause you any problems, I just want to love you. I want to shower you all my love, affection, and attention. The last woman I was with, she didn't appreciate me. I gave her all she could dream of and all she could ask for. In return she gave me nothing, she couldn't love me the way I loved her, she couldn't love me at all. She was a beautiful person; she just did not have the capacity to love anyone."

Vici reached across the table and touched his cheek, she said "Bryan I will never do you like that. I am capable of love, I'm just so used to being used and mistreated that I'm afraid that I may shadow that on to you. Trust me, that's not what I want. I want to love and I definitely want to be loved. So if you promise to help to be patient with me, to help me and to trust me, I promise to try my best to love you the right way."

Bryan put out his pinky to Vici and smiled, she reached her pinky out to him, they interlocked fingers and made a pinky promise.

IVYON

After my trip and talking to Vici about Bryan, I have decided to claim my man, if he'll still have me. I'm going to stop being such a hard ass, put all the bullshit to the side, because at the end of the day, I know that this man really loves me. Ivyon had planned an entire day for her and Rufus. They would start their day with breakfast, followed by private 1 hour long massages, mani and pedi's. Soon after they would have lunch, followed by a boat ride, and a movie. Later that evening she would cook him dinner, they would soak in her Jacuzzi and she would give him ultimately the best night of his life yet to come.

Ivyon began her plan by cancelling all his work for the next two days. That same evening, she gave him a call.

"Hello my love."

"Uhm, your voice is like sweet music to my ears. When did you come back? I've missed you so much."

"I just landed a couple of hours ago. I've missed you too, that's why I couldn't wait to call you."

"I just love the sound of your voice. Did you get some rest yet?'

"No, I wasn't too tired. I got in, cooked me something to eat and had a glass of wine while I unpacked and put away my clothes that I didn't use and bagged the one's that I did to send off to the cleaner's. I soon grew tired of that and I wanted something to lift my spirits, so I called you."

"Well I'm glad you did. As bad as I wanted to, I couldn't bring myself to call and disturb your trip. I couldn't think of anything or anyone else but you. I hardly scheduled any surgeries while you were gone. I just couldn't get it together without my girl here. I know we're going through a rough patch Ivy, but God knows I love you. He put me here for you and no one else."

"I know Rufus, and I love you too. We'll get through this, I know we will. If you don't mind, I've made plans for us for tomorrow; I hope that you'll like it. Tomorrow is a day reserved just for us."

"Ivy, I'm booked up in the hospital tomorrow, I'm even on call. Can we do it another day? Don't get me wrong, I would give the world to be able to spend time with you."

"Oh don't worry about that honey, I've taken care of all that, your schedule is cleared."

"Oh really? Well excuse me Ms. Ivyon Moore. I guess I'm free tomorrow, then."

"Yes, you are Mr. Doctor. Well you go ahead and get some rest. I'll see you in the morning."

"What time should I be ready?"

"Around 7 is good."

"7? Really?

"Yes our day starts around 8 and then we'll go from there."

"Ok, so should I be at your house at 8?"

"No, let me take care of all of that. Tomorrow is about you. Just be ready by 7."

With Ivyon disconnected her call, took a shower and went to bed ready for her day with Rufus tomorrow. She was so excited, she could hardly sleep.

What she didn't know was that Tina had somehow tapped into her phone, so now she knew that Ivyon would be out of house tomorrow at least by 7. The next morning, Ivyon wrote out her itinerary for the day of her plans with Rufus. She had everything planned out from breakfast until dinner. Ivyon was dressed and inside her Pearly Pink Jaguar headed to Rufus' house at 7; she could only hope that he was dressed and ready to go, because she certainly was.

Ivyon pulled up to Rufus' house and to her surprise, he was waiting on the porch for her. His face lit up with love as soon as he saw her pull into his driveway. He walked out to the driver's side of her car, leaned in the window and kissed her. He drew back, rubbed her cheek and said "I love you." Ivyon could do nothing but smile, she was in love and she knew it, all she wanted to do was be with this man at whatever cost. Rufus got into the car and Ivyon kissed him passionately, looked deep into his eyes and pulled off to start their day. Ivyon took Rufus down to Annapolis on the water to a nice, secluded breakfast nook where they enjoyed each other's company over fresh fruits, mimosa, and blueberry waffles. They couldn't have wanted for anything else, just to be in each other's presence was enough.

After breakfast, Ivyon drove them to Hershey for a day at the spa. They both enjoyed a 1 hour chocolate wrap/massage, followed shortly by fresh greens, fruit and grilled chicken salad. Again they basked in each other's presence. After lunch they walked around for a few hours just enjoying the sights and each other. The next thing on the agenda was dinner, which Ivyon would cook at home and serve him like a King.

Dinner was simple. She made him shrimp scampi over a bed of angel hair pasta with garlic bread on the side, a chilled glass of white Merlot. They ate dinner talking about nothing in particular and laughing. Getting lost in time but it didn't matter to them, they loved each other and they were with each other.

After dinner, Ivyon gave Rufus a nice hot candlelit bubble bath where she straddle him in the tub and gave him the ride of his life, causing crashing waves; water was everywhere, all over the floor and everything. She didn't care, her inside waves were crashing as well. Rufus thrust his pelvis catching Ivyon's rhythm creating their musical affair. They were in an orgasmic combustion, holding tight onto each other, breathing so heavy, and barely catching their breaths. After their exhausting session, they got in the shower together; enjoyed the sights of one another, no one even spoke a word. They got to the bedroom where Ivyon sat Rufus down in her chaise lounge chair, dropped down to one, she pulled out a red Cartier box from behind her back and she asked the infamous words

"Rufus, will you do me the honor of being my husband?"

Rufus looked at Ivyon, grabbed her by the elbows to help her up, he kissed her with so much passion and said "Yes". Ivyon if you hadn't asked me tonight, I would have asked you. He got up and walked over to his clothes, he also pulled out a Cartier box, inside was a 3 carat, heart shaped single diamond. They accepted their rings together while

Ivyon cried and just before they could embrace in a kiss, Ivyon's walk-in closet doors swung open, "YOU WILL NOT MARRY HIM AFTER ALL I'VE DONE TO GET YOU."

"Tina? Rufus said in confusion. What the fuck are you doing here?"

"What am I doing here? What the fuck are you doing here? I thought I got rid of you last year when you fucked me in your office? I guess that wasn't enough to make Ivyon stay away from you. What the fuck else do I have to do? Enraged, Tina raised her hand toward Rufus holding a gun. "I guess I have to kill you then."

By this time Ivyon had made her way to her closet to get her gun, she saw that Tina was putting a gun at Rufus an without notice, Ivyon shot her 3 times in the back. Rufus ran over to Ivyon and snatched the gun from her and asked if she was alright. Ivyon was in shock, and just fell to the ground. Rufus grabbed the phone and dialed 911 as he ran over to Tina trying to apply pressure to the wounds. Tina was bleeding profusely; it was nothing Rufus could do. EMS and the police arrived on the scene while Rufus explained to them what had taken place. They wanted to take Ivyon down for questioning, but Rufus wouldn't hear of it, He informed them that she was in shock and they could question her tomorrow at the hospital.

Ivyon allowed Rufus to take her to the hospital where they evaluated her. Ivyon was fine, she was a little shaken up because she'd just killed someone, but she was just relieved that all of this mess was finally over. Neither Rufus nor Ivyon could understand what the hell had happened, what they did understand and was thankful for was the fact that they were alive together.

THE END

Ivyon had barricaded herself in Rufus' house for the last two weeks since she'd shot Tina, she couldn't go back to her house, knowing that she had taken someone's life there. Ivyon was still shaken up; she couldn't believe what had happened. She couldn't believe just how obsessed and crazy Tina really was. She had only heard about stuff like this happening in the movies, never would she had imagined that this would pan out to be her life. One thing that Tina had said to her was true, "you can't just sleep around with people when you want and think nothing will come of it." That rang so true at this point of time with Ivyon, she never thought that pleasing someone and having someone please her would turn out this way.

Ivyon closed everyone out since that incident had occurred, she didn't want to talk to anyone nor did she want to see anyone. The only person she felt save with was Rufus. Rufus had taken some time off work to be with Ivyon, to support her mentally and physically. Ivyon didn't want to eat or anything, all she wanted to do was sleep. She fell asleep in Rufus' arms every day and woke up there as well. He made sure that she at least drank broth and plenty of water to keep her hydrated and somewhat strong. He couldn't stand to see her down like this, his patients, he knew what to do for them but the love of his life; it was as if he had no clue. All he could do was be there for her in any way possible.

Rufus knew that she wouldn't want to go back to her house; too much had happened there, so he would make her stay with him. After the investigation was over, Rufus took it upon himself and had everything either cleaned or replaced. He had her snow-white carpet taken up in her room and replaced with new carpet, anything that blood splatter was on, he threw out and had it replaced. The only thing he could throw out and have replaced was her thoughts, feelings, emotions, and sanity. He completely had her entire bedroom redone with different colors, different furniture, different everything. Anything that would help ease her mind and try to push the memories aside, he did.

Rufus came home after being at her house to oversee the newest project. As soon as he walked in the house he smelled food cooking in the kitchen. He walked in the kitchen and found Ivyon in there making them dinner.

"Ivy, how are you feeling today?"

"I'm fine honey. How are you?"

I'm okay. I'm surprised to see you up and cooking. Do you want me to do that for you while you get some rest?"

Ivyon walked over to Rufus, cupped his cheek, kissed his lips and said "Baby, I'm fine now. She can't do no more harm to me!"

Rufus was surprised at her reaction, but also happy about it. He didn't want this to consume her and take over their life. She had already been through so much; she didn't need any more stress added to her plate. Rufus wished he could just erase all the bad memories that she had, wash her mind completely away of them all. All he wanted to do was be there for her, make her feel safe and love her.

"That's good baby, I'm glad you feel that way. What are you cooking?"

"Stuffed tilapia, topped with lobster in a white cream sauce, with a side of roasted garlic and peppercorn broccoli and cauliflower, and an added pleasure of homemade garlic bread."

"Wow, that's awesome. Are you sure you don't need any help?"

Rufus walked over to the kitchen sink, rolled up his sleeves to wash his hands.

"Baby, I got it. I'm okay; you don't have to worry about me."

"Well can I at least set the table?"

"Yes, please."

Rufus set the table, pulled out some candles and pour them both a glass of wine to sip on while they waited for dinner to be done. They made small talk and laughed with each other, just admiring each other. Once dinner was ready, Rufus refilled their glasses, lit the candles and prayed over the food before they sat down to eat.

"Ivyon, I've had some work done to your house. I had the carpet taken up and I had everything thrown away and replaced. I'd love to take you over there to show you or I could just show you the pictures if you'd like."

"Rufus, thank you for doing that, but I don't want to see it. I don't even want the house anymore. I mean we're engaged now so I can just move here with you, or we can buy another house and call it ours. We'll sell my house, fully furnished and just be done with it."

"Wow, Ivy I would have never thought you would want to leave your house, your house is awesome. But if that's what you want then that's what we'll do. We can sell mine too and like you said just get a new one. Have it built from the ground up and modeled the way we want, that way it'll have a piece of both of us. For instance, this kitchen and dining room, we'll definitely need a bigger kitchen for my lovely chef."

"See, now you're talking my language, it will be wonderful. We'll sell both houses. When do you want to start looking for a new one? After we sell one of them or ASAP?"

"That's up to you sweetie, whatever you wantt."

"Well let's start looking now. Why wait?"

Ivyon was acting a little too well for Rufus, but if she said she was ok, then he would leave it at that. All he was worried about was being with her, and now he finally was.

"Babe, we haven't had the time to celebrate our engagement. Would you like it if I threw us a party and invited everyone over? I know you miss everyone. You haven't seen Vici or your family since you left Dubai, and we haven't had the chance to tell anyone our great news."

"I don't know if I'm ready to see everyone yet. I've been through so much this year; I just want to be with you."

"Ivy, you just told me that you were fine, now you're telling me that you don't know if you're ready to see everyone? Come on now babe, you are much stronger than that and you know you are."

"How do you know how strong I am Rufus? You know nothing about me."

"I know that you have been through a whole hell of a lot throughout your life, I know that almost everyone in your life, including me has let you down at some point, I know that above everything that I've mentioned and all that I haven't you have still found a way to climb to the top of it all and showed everyone that you would not let anyone get in your way or stop you. I may not know everything about you, but I know enough to know that you are strong and you can overcome anything. I know all I need to know about you Ivy, I know that I love you and that's all I need to know; unless, of course, you want me to know anything else."

Ivyon looked at Rufus with confusion in her eyes, but at the same time, relief. She was relieved at the fact that she didn't have to tell Rufus all of her horror stories, that she didn't have to go into detail about how she was addicted to sex from both males and females, how she was sexually involved with Vici for years, but also l kept her as her best friend. She was RELIEVED.

"Okay Rufus should we have a small dinner here or should we go all out and have a BIG party?"

"I think we should have a BIG party. We'll send out invitations and rent out a space somewhere. I think it would take your mind off things honey."

Ivyon looked at Rufus and smiled. She got up from the table, clearing their dishes away so they could lie across the couch with some popcorn to watch movies. Instead of watching movies, they talked about their party. They talked about who they would invite, what color scheme they would go with, what would be on the menu, etc., they even picked out and ordered their invitations and a date for that next weekend. At the end of the night, Ivyon was excited that Rufus suggested that they celebrate their engagement.

~~~*~~~

Ivyon and Rufus decided to just invite everyone over to his house to celebrate in their love. They had a huge dinner spread that Ivyon prepared herself, even down to the drinks and dinner rolls. They had baked chicken, baked fish, fried chicken, fried fish, spear ribs, ham, an oven roaster, mashed potatoes, string beans, broccoli, corn on the cob, Swedish meatballs, chicken Parmesan, dinner rolls, lemon pound cake, double chocolate cake, strawberry marble cake, banana pudding, the list went on. Not to mention the drinks that she provided.

After everyone had eaten, they all enjoyed each other's company, engaging in conversation about any and everything. Everyone was there, her dad, Tessia, Bronte, Vici and Bryan, some of Rufus' friends and close coworker's and Ivyon loved it. Ivyon took her parents and knocked on her glass with it to get everyone's attention.

"Hello everyone, I wanted to thank all of you personally for coming to celebrate with Rufus and I. You are the most important people to us, so it was only right that you share in our happiness."

"Tell us the story."

Ivyon looked around the room to see who had shouted that out. It was Bronte, her loving sister. Ivyon wrestled with the idea of telling them the story of how they proposed to each other and Tina ruined their night with her bullshit. Rufus noticed Ivyon's face from across the room when she was asked that question, he quickly chimed in,

"Well Ivyon planned an entire day for us to spend together. We had breakfast, then we had a spa day together, lunch, a long walk on the water with a little shopping in between, before we came home and she cooked me the best meal I've ever had in my life. Then we had a nice long bubble bath, I won't tell you what followed. Before I knew it, my girl was actually down on one knee proposing to me. I couldn't believe it, we actually were thinking the same thing. Before I even
answered her, I walked over to my clothes, pulled out my box, opened and said, if you didn't ask me, I was going to ask you. We both said yes, so here we are."

Ivyon was grateful to and for Rufus; he had saved her day once again. Vici noticed how Ivyon reacted to the question so and felt as though that wasn't the entire story. She figured she would just ask her later. She didn't want to put any more pressure on her in front of everyone. They all congratulated Ivyon and Rufus on their new engagement; they asked all sorts of questions about the wedding. When the date was, where they would hold it, what were their colors, etc? It went on for hours before they started "game night". Ivyon had all sorts of games from Candy Land, Monopoly, Spades, Operation, whatever you could think of, they had it. After Rufus' friends and coworker's left, Vici felt more comfortable asking them what really happened. Rufus' friends and coworker's weren't a part of their circle so they didn't need to know what was really going on. They were all sitting around the table enjoying glasses of wine and other alcoholic beverages, laughing in conversation when Vici said,

"Ok you guys, there is obviously more to that story, why don't you tell us what really happened?"

"What do you mean Vici?"

"Come on Rufus, I saw the way you looked at Ivy when she kind of froze up before you told the story. It was a lovely story but it just seems like you guys left something out. Ivy, why did you freeze up and let Rufus answer for you?"

"Vici , I think you're crossing the line now. What I said is what happened."

"Rufus, it's ok. If anyone here knows me, Vici does. She's right there is more to the story."

"Honey we didn't have this party for that, we had it to celebrate and to clear your mind."

"I know that, but I have to get it off my chest. I have to talk about it eventually and everyone here is family, y'all love me and I love y'all. What Rufus told y'all was correct, the only part that he didn't mention was that to our surprise, Tina's crazy ass was hiding in my closet and once I accepted Rufus' proposal, she bust in with a gun. She was screaming about how I couldn't marry him how she thought she had gotten rid of him when she fucked him in his office. Since none of that worked, she threatened to kill him. So while Rufus was talking to her, I ran over to my closet, grabbed my gun and I shot her. I didn't intend to but she was there in my house again, this time trying to kill me and the man I love. The crazy part is that she had been stalking me ever since I met her. It was like she knew my every move, as if she would meet me wherever I was. Can you believe that she was actually in Dubai when we were there?"

"Oh my God Ivy, are you ok?" Vici asked mostly out of concern and mainly out of anger. She felt helpless because there was nothing she could have done. Nothing that she did do, she was holding that against herself because most of all, she was supposed to have been Ivyon's best friend. All of this was going on right under her nose.

"Yes Vici, I'm okay. Thanks for asking."

"Well Ivyon where did you meet this girl, what does she look like?" Tessia asked.

"I met her a few years ago at a nightclub and I'd been dealing with her off and on since then. But when Rufus and I got together, I stopped dealing with her and I guess that was a problem. Shortly after she tricked Rufus into sleeping with her in hopes that I would leave Rufus alone and come back to her. That didn't work, so she started stalking me. She broke into my house one night and tied me up and sexually assaulted me, I shot her that night also. I thought that was the end of her when that happened, then I got a call from her while we were in Dubai. She was there; I mean she told me everything that I was wearing, down to how I had my hair. But again, I brushed her off. I guess I just thought that she would leave me alone."

"Wait. You said it's the same girl that you shot?"

"Yes Bronte, I told you about that."

Bronte's wheels in her head started to turn. She was thinking back to that night. She remembered trying to get in touch with Samone that night and she told her she couldn't see her, that she wasn't feeling good. Then after that she kept asking about Ivyon, she acted as if she wanted to have three-sum with her. She was acting obsessed.

"Ivyon do you have a picture of her?"

"I doubt it; I mean I haven't been involved with her for years. I mean what difference does it make you guys?"

"Ivyon I didn't mean to upset you, I was just wondering that's all."

"Well she's about my height, of course she not unattractive; if she was I wouldn't have been with her."

Ivyon started looking through her phone to see if she may have had an older picture of her or not. Unbeknownst to her, she did have one. She showed her phone around the room to everyone showing them what Tina looked like. Once her phone reached Bronte, she starred at the picture, jumped to her feet and her phone hit the floor causing the screen to shatter.

"Bronte, what the hell is wrong with you? Why'd you drop my phone?"

Bronte just looked at Ivyon covering her mouth in pure shock, she couldn't utter a word. Everyone looked at her in confusion before Vici finally said, "Bronte is this girl you were talking about in Dubai?"

"Vici what are you talking about? I never told you that I was involved with a woman or anyone for that matter."

Bronte quickly dropped her head trying to get the attention off of her.

"Bronte, why and how did you just break my goddamn phone? Bronte?"

"Ivyon I didn't mean to, I saw this girl on the news and just couldn't believe that she was the one you were talking about."

"Bronte as your sister, I'm going to ask you to stop lying to me and to tell me what you know about this woman."

"Ivyon, what are you talking about? I do not know her."

Bronte had fear in her eyes. Just couldn't bring herself to tell Ivyon that the woman that caused her so much pain, the one that stalked her, the one that sexually assaulted her, was the one that had her mind gone, the one that had turned her out, the one that she wanted to be with.

Ivyon walked over to Bronte, cupped her chin and lifted her head. She saw a tear roll down her sisters' face.

"Bronte, it's okay. You didn't know. I know you never bring me any harm. Tina was a manipulator, she could make you do things that you didn't want to."

Tears streamed down her face; Bronte was trying to apologize to Ivyon.

"Ivyon, I'm so sorry. I didn't know that she was the one that was doing that to you. I met her in the parking garage of the mall, I had no idea. Believe me please. I never even knew her name was Tina, she told me her name was Samone.

Everyone sat back in shock listening to all the details unfold. They couldn't believe what they were hearing.

Rufus was the one that was a little more confused than the rest, but he caught on pretty quick.

"Ivyon this is crazy. Are you sure you killed her because I didn't hear about it on the news? If she didn't die, you definitely need a restraining order against her." Everyone turned their attention to Rufus.

"Rufus, did I kill her????"